Abandoned

A Vietnam War Love Story

By

Gary L Gresh

****

****

*

This story is a work of fiction

**

The story is written in the language of the time.

***

Any resemblance to actual persons, living or dead, or actual events is purely coincidental.

DEDICATION

To everyone who served in the Vietnam War:

Volunteer or Draftee; they went when called and their lives have never been the same since that day.

PREFACE:

Who or what would you think about if you were wounded in combat and left abandoned in enemy territory to fend for yourself in rugged terrain with only your pistol and a knife as weapons for protection?

Would you strike out on your own toward a friendly location, or would you stay and wait for rescue from a force that might never come?

Army Lieutenant Adam Duke Gabriel had to make that decision when he found himself wounded and abandoned by his unit when they thought he was dead.

His actions, his strengths, his faith, and his very mental stability would soon be tested as never tested before. It would also lead him back to the love of his life and give him the future he had always envisioned.

FORWARD:
1964

Adam Duke Gabriel joined the Reserve Officers Training Corps (ROTC) in College for three reasons:

1st, he respected the military and thought that he should serve his country just like his father and grandfather had done before him.

2nd, he was a realist and knew that he would eventually be drafted for the Vietnam War if he did not step up and volunteer.

3rd, he could use the $100 a month pay that was offered by ROTC and wanted to serve his country as an officer, not as an enlisted man as his father had done.

Once joining freshman ROTC at the University of Texas in Austin, Texas; 'Adam', known as 'Duke' by his friends, learned that a two-year ROTC scholarship might also be available if he applied. It would pay basic tuition for his junior and senior years if he could meet the grades and writing requirements, and if he was willing to go on active duty in the army immediately upon graduation.

His parents, while financially comfortable, could still use the help with the cost of his college tuition, so 'Duke' applied and won an Army Two-Year ROTC Scholarship for his junior and senior years. Most family ranches in the state of Texas were sinkholes for expenses all of the time, and Duke wanted to help his parents with the extra cost involved for his college education. It would be his way of helping them out while still obtaining his degree.

Adam's middle name "Duke' was given to him by his father because his father was an ardent fan of the great western actor John Wayne. His son, Duke, always tried hard to live up to that persona. Duke had spent his entire life growing up on the family ranch and was a true cowboy through and through.

Duke was an unusual young man in the 1960's, as he was very mature for his age, religious, and not easily swayed by drugs, alcohol, or the rebellious attitudes and contemporary political thoughts shared by many of his teenaged friends. His mother called him an "Old Soul", but she smiled when she said it.

Upon graduation from college, he entered the United States Army as planned, and then sought out every challenging school the US Army offered to each officer. Duke fancied himself a tough guy and so he volunteered for Ranger and Airborne Training. He had excelled in several sports in both high school and college and had been the bigger than life quarterback on his high school football team. He knew that the Army Ranger and Airborne training courses would be both challenging and rewarding. He was absolutely right about that on both counts.

Duke courted and eventually married Miss. Faith Anderson during his final year in College. They married soon after their engagement because Faith wanted to be as close to Adam as possible while he was serving his country in Vietnam. She knew that being his wife would give her better access to critical information should he be wounded or injured in the war and she did not want to be shut out.

Adam left Fort Benning, Georgia on 10 August 1969 headed for Vietnam. His orders took him to the in-processing center located on Bien Hoa Air Force Base, Vietnam. The Army's Individual Replacement System in Vietnam provided fighting men for the various combat units on an "as needed" basis. This meant that officers and enlisted personnel were sent to the various units based on replacement needs and the individual qualifications needed by the individual units.

Duke was considered a highly qualified infantry candidate because he was an Airborne Ranger trained Infantry Officer. He also had already served six months as an aide-de-camp to a general officer, which meant that his file was highly rated by the in-processing folks in Vietnam.

He was immediately singled out to go to the 101st Airborne Airmobile Division at Camp Eagle, I Corps, in Vietnam. The 101st Division was currently operating near the city of Hue in northern South Vietnam. Duke would eventually be assigned as an infantry platoon leader in an infantry company assigned to the 1/327th Infantry Battalion.

He was quickly transported to the Infantry Battalion's rear area location, which was near Firebase Bastogne, in I Corps, Vietnam, near the northern mountains of South Vietnam. Within just two weeks of arriving in Vietnam, Duke was now sitting in the jungle just outside Firebase Bastogne as the 1st Platoon leader, D Company, 1/327th Infantry.

He had already written two letters back to his wife of only six months, "Faith", telling her of his travels through the replacement officer system to his current position. He was proud to be assigned to the 101st Airborne Division because of its legendary history from WWII. He was very busy getting to know all of his soldiers and his new Platoon Sergeant.

He soon learned that the next twelve months were going to be long, hard, and hot! Vietnam exceeded every expectation he had expected. But the heat and rain were both beyond his wildest expectations. How in the world did anyone live in this climate? Even the Texas heat and the Texas rains were no match for this Godforsaken country. It was going to be a long year!

Duke had an active duty obligation of four years, and he had known from the beginning that service in Vietnam was going to be part of that obligation. He would serve his obligation and then return to the Double Star Ranch in Texas for the rest of his life. That was the plan. But The Vietnam War had a way of changing many a well intentioned plan!

Table of Contents:

Chapter One: Abandoned

First Platoon, D Company, 1/327th Infantry
101st Airborne Airmobile Division
Republic of Vietnam
April 1970

First Lieutenant Adam Duke Gabriel was now considered to be a seasoned platoon leader in the 101st Airborne, Airmobile Division, presently assigned to I Corps, Republic of Vietnam. He had deployed from the United State in August 1969 and had been assigned to the 101st Airborne Airmobile Division, serving in I Corps in Northern South Vietnam near the DMZ (Demilitarized Zone).

He had been in the country of Vietnam for over eight months now, and was very comfortable in his role as the leader of some twenty-six men in his combat platoon. His mission was 'to close with and destroy the enemy', but the mental and physical mechanics of such a mission had recently become much more difficult.

The enemy only struck when they had overwhelmingly favorable odds or from a distance using mortars or booby traps for which there was little defense. Duke had 'closed with the enemy' and had taken hill after hill in Vietnam, only to return the territory back to the enemy when they left that hill to attack some other hill.

Duke had become somewhat jaded, as he strongly felt that the war was being mismanaged by the political leadership in the USA. He believed that they had tied the hands of the military leaders because of their insistence that the military fight only a 'defensive type' war in Vietnam.

Imaginary lines had been drawn all over Vietnam using the geographical parallels of Latitude and Longitude, over which the military could not venture. Therefore, the military was fighting the war with limited military resources and limited goals. It was as if the military fighting force had one hand tied behind their back.

But such political goals and intrigue were all above the pay grade of First Lieutenant Duke Gabriel. His problem was much closer to home, his own platoon. He had to keep the morale of twenty-six soldiers high and had to show a strong leadership presence which must include no criticism whatsoever of any higher authority.

His ranger qualification training and his famed 'Ranger Tab' had automatically given him immense respect, as the Ranger Tab worn by every ranger was very well thought of among the soldiers of the US Army. The army rangers had first gained great respect during WWII when led by the famed Lieutenant Colonel William O. Darby in the North African Campaign under General Patton's Army. The army had later created the Ranger Course at Fort Benning, Georgia, for young combat leaders, and anyone graduating with the one half of each class that was awarded the coveted Ranger Tab, was given the almost automatic credentials of a superior leader.

Duke wore his ranger-patrolling cap under his steel helmet. That meant that everyone was reminded daily of his training and background whenever he took a break and took off the steel helmet exposing the famed ranger cap with its prominent Ranger Tab sewn on the front.

Duke tried hard to keep his rather strong opinions about the war and how it was being fought to himself, and just tried to keep his soldiers alive to return back home to their families. He, like many other lieutenants in the Vietnam War, had eventually adopted somewhat more defensive posture, as he had long ago learned that losing soldiers to useless assaults was an exercise in futility. The hilltop taken from the enemy today was just as quickly returned to the enemy tomorrow when his unit left the area. It was very frustrating.

But lately, the mission of keeping his soldiers safe and alive had become much more difficult. The newspapers and letters from home brought news of the many demonstrations against the war in the streets of the USA. These same stories both eroded trust in the military and emboldened the very enemy they were fighting here in Vietnam.

The past month of March 1970 had been the hottest and most active fighting month of the war to date. Duke had certainly noticed the recent ramping up of the enemy contacts, resistance, and harassment of the US troops in his area of operations. The more public the debate about the war became in the states, the heavier the action seemed to get here in Vietnam.

The enemy knew that the U.S. people and their deployed soldiers were all tired of the war. The communists felt they could outwait the U.S. troop units, as eventually the U.S. Army would just leave, like the French Army had done before them. The war in Indochina was always a waiting game to the ever-patient communists of North Vietnam.

The demonstrations in the USA just emboldened the enemy. The North Vietnamese Army had gone on an aggressive offense using small unit guerrilla forces to intimidate the US Forces by striking units using mortars and booby-traps from afar. Such quick hit and run guerrilla attacks by very small units caused major demoralization of the US Forces, while preserving the strength of the North Vietnamese Army (NVA) forces operating in South Vietnam.

Duke had become quite adept at avoiding the enemy mortar attacks, but he knew it was probably just a matter of time before a mortar round would hit close enough to his platoon to cause some casualties. Duke did everything in his power to avoid such attacks by firing artillery rounds on adjacent hilltops as his unit moved through the jungle when friendly forces locations allowed. But sometimes, he could not use the artillery because of the dense jungle which obscured his vision, or when he was unsure whether there were any other friendly forces operating in his area of operations.

It seemed that lately, the enemy had withdrawn major forces from his area of operations. Sometimes, the NVA left behind small guerilla groups of highly trained Sapper (Engineer) soldiers. Their mission was to set up explosive booby traps and also to mortar US Units from afar when U.S. unit locations were known. This tactic had been used many times in the last month. In fact, the intent of the enemy had become so predictable, that Duke had requested and received a scout dog and handler to walk point with his platoon.

The dog and his handler had been a tremendous help in detecting 'booby traps', (explosive devices) set up on the various trails in the jungle. The scout dog always found any explosive device well before any member of Duke's platoon would trip the wire used to detonate the bomb. The dog had already saved lives several times in Duke's unit in just the past twenty days.

But the most dangerous times of late for his platoon had become the insertion or extraction of his platoon from any landing zone (LZ). These insertions and extractions used the 'Huey' helicopters of the 101st Division. Those helicopters were so plentiful in the division but were also very noisy as they arrived or departed. Everyone in the jungle within a mile of any LZ being landed upon could easily hear the helicopters arriving and departing from the LZ. You just could not silence the noise of the giant green flying machines.

It was for that very reason that Duke had spread the twenty-six soldiers of his First Platoon, D Company out over 100 meters as they approached the LZ on Hill 786. He did not want them 'bunched-up' next to the LZ from which they were about to be extracted from this morning. By spreading out his men he at least diminished the size of his platoon as a possible target for enemy mortars, should an enemy unit be nearby this morning.

His company commander, Captain Barclay, had decided this morning to move Duke's platoon to another area much later today. The past week his platoon had not encountered any enemy forces in this area. His platoon was currently operating in the thick jungle about fifteen clicks (Kilometers) from Firebase Veghel. Captain Barclay had decided that the enemy just did not seem to be in this area of operations at this time and that his troops were not currently being used to their best advantage.

The battalion and company commanders had both decided to move some units to another side of Firebase Veghel to keep any potential enemy away from the battalion headquarters currently on the firebase. This meant repositioning D Company and its platoons to the mountains northwest of the firebase from the mountains northeast of the firebase, where they were currently operating.

Duke often spread his soldiers apart when approaching any LZ, just in case the enemy should decide to mortar the LZ once the helicopters came to pick up the troops. Duke felt that these simple tactical maneuvers he constantly used might save some soldiers someday if his platoon was ever attacked while being extracted by helicopters.

Duke was currently standing on the LZ in front of his platoon late that afternoon and planned to control the loading of the helicopters (birds) as they arrived, usually two at a time, to pick up his troops. His platoon sergeant, SFC Bell, would leave the area with a squad of soldiers on the first two birds. The second set of birds would pick up the next squad and this would continue until all four squads and the platoon leader were extracted from the LZ well before dark.

Duke would go out with the last squad on the final two birds. This provided leadership at both ends of the extraction process and left the platoon leader on the LZ to call for artillery fires should it become necessary during the extraction to protect the birds and his platoon members. Since the new area of operations was unknown to the enemy, it was more likely that any attack would occur here, where the enemy already knew where the US units were located, than at the new LZ where they were about to be inserted.

Duke pulled the safety pin on a green smoke grenade and threw the grenade on top of the LZ right in front of him. The green smoke started to curl up into the air to identify the friendly LZ location for the incoming helicopter pilots. Within seconds, the incoming helicopters started to land and pick up his soldiers. Everything was going as planned until the last two birds arrived to pick up Duke and his Radio Telephone Operator (RTO) along with the last squad of six men.

Just as the last two birds started to turn into the LZ, lifting their front ends to come in for a landing, the hair on Duke's arms rose. That uncontrollable physical reaction was always an indicator to Duke of impending danger! He immediately looked around the LZ for any dangers that might be present. He saw none.

He and Corporal Turner, his RTO, were standing beside the first bird as it landed on the cleared pad of the LZ. Everything after that moment in time appeared to happen in microseconds, not minutes, and would be seared into Duke's memory forever.

The last two birds were being quickly loaded with soldiers when the first two enemy mortar rounds impacted onto the LZ between the two helicopters currently loading out his troops. Lieutenant Gabriel swung his arm around his RTO, Corporal Tim Turner and pushed him to the ground, as he himself went to the ground.

The helicopter pilots immediately reacted to the incoming rounds by lifting off the LZ in an attempt to evade the rounds. The pilots wanted to save their birds and soldiers from the incoming rounds, which were now impacting all around them. Squad members were trying to get into the birds at the same time as the pilots were trying to take off. Soldiers were hanging on to the helicopter skids and doorways. It was total pandemonium!

Duke had not even loaded his helicopter yet, as he was standing beside the bird with his RTO, motioning for troops to load. At that very moment, before Duke could even reach for his radio handset, as he now lay on the ground, the entire landing zone went up in flames as both helicopters exploded in huge fireballs, spewing fuel, bodies, and shrapnel in all directions. It was a devastating and massive explosion.

The combined explosions of the helicopters, the mortars, and even some of the ammunition carried by his soldiers, became mind-boggling and completely disastrous. Bodies, shrapnel, helicopter parts, and raging fuel fires exploded in every direction. Duke and his RTO were literally blown off the LZ by the force of the explosions, both thrown more than 100 feet off the LZ and over a 200-foot drop off the edge of the mountain on which the LZ was located.

Mortar rounds continued to plummet onto the LZ from the air above and soon the entire hilltop was engulfed in flames and total destruction. The bulk of the first platoon had already left the area, and they currently had no idea of what had just transpired back at the extraction LZ. It took almost ten minutes for the company commander to realize what had just happened to the last element of his first platoon. It would then take yet another hour to get any rescue helicopters and forces into the air to return to the site of the explosions on the extraction LZ.

When the 1/327th Infantry rescue forces finally returned to the location of the explosions on the LZ on Hill 786, they found no enemy soldiers, no trace of an enemy mortar team, and the total destruction of all forces that had been on the LZ, including the two helicopters, the fourth squad of First Platoon, D Company, 1/327th Infantry and its command team.

There was barely anything left on the LZ bigger than a rucksack and a lot of blood, bones, and charred bodies were spread everywhere. A search of the paths into the jungle where the platoon had staged turned up a few individual items of clothing and a couple of canteens and rucksacks, but no living soul could be found anywhere near the LZ.

After searching the area for almost an hour, the rescue force finally called for extraction and out-loaded body bags containing many body parts and assorted weapons from the devastating explosion site. The rescue force then left the area before the enemy could regroup and attack the LZ again. It would take another week to discover that none of the bodies or body parts gathered that day appeared to belong to First Lieutenant Duke Gabriel or his RTO, Corporal Tim Turner.

Most soldiers could not be easily identified because they were so badly burned and forensics teams would have to be used to determine who was who among the pieces of human remains, or even if perhaps several members of the platoon had actually been totally incinerated by the flames.

In the meantime, unknown to anyone in the 1/327th Infantry, First Lieutenant Duke Gabriel was presently wounded, burned, abandoned, alive, and unconscious in a ditch down the hill from all of the devastation on the LZ above on Hill 786.

Chapter Two: Faith Anderson
(Two Years Prior)
1968

Faith Anderson was a Texas country girl through and through. She was a blue-eyed blond that had a striking appearance and carried herself well. She was shy, very intelligent, and self-assured. The fact that she had grown to be a real beauty was a plus.

She was raised in San Angelo, Texas, by middle-class parents that instilled both strong values and an abiding faith in God. Faith was just one of four siblings, all having a strong work ethic and desire to excel. All four kids were active in high school sports, the Four-H Club and their church. The family owned a small Feed and Seed store in San Angelo, Texas, that had been in the family for three generations. It was expected that the children would inherit the store and the family ethic that it maintained.

Faith and her three siblings, Hope, Charity, and Alex, all dated throughout high school, but Faith had only ever met one boy that really turned her head. That boy was named Duke Gabriel, but he was evidently not meant to be her forever-after lover. They had a couple of dates in high school but the relationship never really blossomed at that time and they both went their separate ways. She had not yet found anyone else that rose to the level of her first infatuation with Duke Gabriel, to become a serious love interest. Duke had touched something deep in Faith, but he was a year younger than Faith and was very immature at the time.

Faith Anderson decided to become a nurse while still in high school because of a prolonged illness that kept her away from her senior year for over three months and caused her to repeat the grade before graduation at age nineteen. At age fifteen she was a Tomboy, who wanted to become a cowgirl, but her sex and slight build eventually persuaded her that becoming a cowgirl would probably not work out. Besides, her family wanted her to help with the store.

The illness that prevented her from finishing her senior year of high school was a very bad case of the flu. It had kept her in bed for almost six weeks and then she was so weak, that she just could not return to school in time to be able to graduate with her class. At the time, there was no way to homeschool, so she had to repeat her senior year. The Flu had given her a reason and eventually her desire to become a nurse. She wanted to help others and had a great desire to also serve her country.

She had decided she wanted to help people like the nurse that lived next door to her family and had helped her, during her illness. She had known for some time that she would like to become a nurse, but the idea of joining the army during the Vietnam War came to her much later from an uncle who had served in Vietnam and had mentioned the many fine army nurses that he had seen in Vietnam. He had told Faith that the soldiers in Vietnam thought that an army nurse was like an angel sent by God for the wounded. That idea had stayed with her forever after she had heard it spoken.

Faith dated several guys in high school and even attended most of the high school dances that were held on almost every holiday. She met Duke Gabriel at a Four H event and then again at several football games held between her high school in San Angelo and his from Odessa, Texas. But she was slightly older than Duke as a high school senior because of her earlier flu, which had kept her back a grade. At any rate, Duke was not interested in becoming serious with any girl in high school, as his only interests in life at the time appeared to be football, cattle, horses, and dogs and not necessarily in any particular order.

Adam Duke Gabriel was nice enough to her, but it was clear that he had no intention of going steady with any girl and when the flu separated her from the football games for over three months in her senior year, Duke quickly lost any interest in Faith Anderson.

The idea of becoming an Army Nurse in the Army Medical Corps also appealed to Faith because of her independent spirit and complete confidence in her ability to serve her country as well as any man. She sought out information from a local recruiter while she was still in high school and before she had entered college in Austin, Texas in 1965. The recruiter told Faith that there were several programs that nurses could pursue to become an army officer.

The Reserve Officer's Training Program (ROTC) common on college campuses, did not allow women members at the time, but the US Army Medical Corps did have an Officer Training Program for women that was completely separate from the normal ROTC and Women's Army Corps (WAC) programs.

Faith was told that she must first obtain her degree in nursing and pass her certification tests to become a registered nurse. Once qualified, the army would accept her application to become an army nurse if she could pass the required army physical and other security and screening requirements. Once accepted into the program, she would then be sent to The Officer Training School run by the Army Medical Corps in San Antonio, Texas for about six weeks.

The Army Medical Officer Training Program in San Antonio was essentially just an orientation program to teach potential nurses army officer etiquette and policies regarding rank and discipline in the army. Nurses were viewed as non-combatants and therefore were given no instruction in weapons, tactics, or leadership. After completing that orientation program, she would be assigned to an army hospital in Vietnam for six months as an army nurse. Once serving her tour in Vietnam, she could then elect to stay in the Army Reserves or leave the service at her discretion. She filed the information away for future consideration. But for now, she had to focus on getting her nursing degree.

The idea of army service appealed to Faith who still had a very strong desire to serve her country. Her mother had been a WAC (Women's Army Corps) member for four years many years ago, and still talked about the adventures she had enjoyed while serving in Europe. Faith entered the four-year college nursing degree program with a firm desire to get her nursing degree and then she might consider applying to the US Army Nursing Program. Maybe the army would send her to Europe so she could see some of the world outside of Texas?

She studied hard and was soon known by her friends as a driven young lady with a firm grasp on her future and the requirements she would need to become a registered nurse. She had also blossomed into a truly beautiful woman that naturally turned heads wherever she went. Her mother thought of Faith as the perfect duckling, small yet gangly, that had actually matured into a beautiful swan. She was so very graceful and her drop dead great looks quickly became the talk of the family. She could just about wear anything and look good in it.

She entered the University of Texas Nursing School in Austin, Texas in 1965, right out of her high school in San Angelo, Texas. She was a still a country girl at heart, and even had her own horse at home and therefore, she did not want to leave Texas to go to college. She loved riding and had participated several times in the barrel racing events at the local rodeos each year. She wanted to be close enough to home to see her horse now and then while attending college.

Faith had even considered majoring in Veterinary Medicine but eventually deferred to nursing, as her true love. Faith was just five foot five inches tall and only weighed a little over 110 pounds. She felt that her small size would have become a hindrance to becoming a good horse doctor because of her weight and ability to physically handle the larger farm animals when they were in pain. She handled her own horse just fine, but 'Wildflower' was such a gentle animal and had never tried to resist her in any way whatsoever.

In the end, Faith selected nursing as her major and entered college in the fall of 1965. She loved college and dated several men while there, but again, no one she dated ever seemed to measure up to her memory of Duke Gabriel back at those early football games in high school. She was not super conservative, and certainly not a prude, but she did consider herself a moderate politically, and an avid believer in female identity and female equality.

Faith was not a party girl and believed earnestly in God. She also believed that her soul mate was out there somewhere, but that she did not think that she had crossed paths with that person as of yet. The kicker in all of this was that Faith was now absolutely beautiful by any measurable standard. She turned men's heads wherever she went and could have easily won almost any beauty contest that she might want to enter.

But she remained oblivious to her own good looks and stunning appearance. She wore blue jeans and simple tops almost daily and even when she dressed up for any occasion, she rarely wore more than a strand of pearls that her parents had given her for her sixteenth birthday.

She avoided joining a sorority in college because most of those girls had money and seemed more intent on finding a husband than finding a career. Faith wanted both, but no man was going to tell her that she could not be a nurse! The man she eventually married would have to be a gentleman who understood her own desire to have a life outside of the home. That did not mean that she would be any less of a woman or mother, but by God, she would not play second fiddle to any man! She wanted a partner for life, not a boss.

She kept comparing all men with Duke Gabriel whom she had dated twice back in high school. Duke was always gentlemanly polite, but he had never tried to run her life, or tell her what to do. In fact, if anything, perhaps he was almost too unconcerned with whatever she wanted to do with her life. But his manly stature, manners, and equal treatment of her had remained with her to this day. She just knew there were men out there more like Duke Gabriel that would be a true equal partner in life; she just had to find her forever-after 'man'.

As her last year in college approached she decided that she wanted to start dating again. She had put dating on the back burner through most of her college years because she was so focused on her degree, but now she missed not having someone with whom she could talk and relate. She sought out her friend Julie Bennett who was always trying to 'Hook her up with a blind date" and asked Julie who she might know that was nice, yet, substantial in nature. Julie had been just waiting for Faith to ask for advice about men and jumped on the chance to set up her friend.

The next several months contained a nonstop string of dates with eligible bachelors that had both failed to meet the grade required by Faith, and actually had a chilling effect on Faith's confidence in men in general. Why were most men just interested in sex, as opposed to wanting to start any lifelong attachment? She wanted a man that was interesting, not just shallow and self-absorbed.

Faith finally told Julie to cease and desist, and that she would have to seek a partner on her own. Julie was slightly miffed, but did understand Faith's resistance to some of the guys that Julie had thought were nice guys but had proved to be a disappointment. Julie had asked Faith to go on the upcoming Senior Spring Break weekend with her to Padre Island, Texas. It would be their last spring together as both would graduate in just a few months. Faith had never gone on a spring break weekend and decided that she should probably try to experience a college spring break before graduating from college.

She asked her parents if they thought it would be OK for her to go with Julie on spring break at Padre Island and they both told her to enjoy her senior year. But they cautioned her to stay with Julie and to not do anything stupid or to drink too much alcohol. Faith had never been a drinker and assured them that she would be OK.

Spring Break at Padre Island was a lot of fun and she and Julie did have a great time together. Faith was the 'Bell of the Ball', as almost every guy liked being seen with her at the various activities set up by the University Nursing Alumni Association. She had to admit that she was having a good time. She was glad that she had come to Padre Island until the very last night when they attended the final beach ball festival and Faith saw Adam Duke Gabriel play volleyball on the Army ROTC team as it fought for the championship against one of the most popular fraternities on campus.

She had not see Duke Gabriel for over three years and he had matured well in that time. His body was sculptured perfectly and his athletic build had attracted several girls who were buzzing around him like honeybees. She sat back on the sand and watched as he played volleyball and laughed with several of his friends. She badly wanted to go up to him and introduce herself, but she refused to play the role of a groupie. It was obvious to Faith that Duke Gabriel certainly did not need her, as two young women were currently both vying for his undivided attention.

She got up off the sand and made her way back to the motel to the room she was sharing with Julie. Her spring break had ended. Duke would now remain an unreachable person in her life. She just did not run in those fast circles. The unfortunate thing about her decision to leave the beach was that Duke Gabriel was presently looking for a way to rid him of the two young women that seemed to have targeted him for conquest.

It was clear that the women were only interested in him because they had heard his family owned a ranch in Odessa, Texas. He did not own the ranch, his father did. His friend and big mouth Bernie Sander had told the women that Duke owned the Double Star Ranch, a well-known beef supplier and had raised their hopes of roping a wealthy husband while on spring break of their senior year. He would never date anyone who was only interested in his possible inheritance instead of his own personality and his own future capabilities.

Duke soon found an excuse to leave the beach party and was presently looking for the woman he had noticed on the beach several hours earlier that had intrigued him because she seemed so shy. The woman he was looking for was Faith Anderson, but she had already left the beach, and he could no longer find her anywhere among the students. He kicked himself. He should have approached her when he had first noticed her sitting alone.

Chapter Three: Day One Alone

Duke Awakens to Misery

Duke woke up and wondered immediately where he was? It was cold, dark, and wet. He struggled to remember anything. His ears hurt and were ringing. He touched his face and found it wet and that it hurt like hell and was blistered. His memory was foggy. He hurt everywhere on his body. His arms were tingling and his eyes were filled with dirt, debris, and tears. He strained to try and see anything to no avail. He tried to move but found any movement at all to be excruciating.

Then it all flooded back to him, the explosions, the fire, the yelling, and the pandemonium. His platoon had been attacked on the LZ using mortar or artillery fire. He remembered thinking that there was a potential danger because the hair on his arms had risen, but it all had happened so fast, he had no time to react to his innate warning system.

He now silently took inventory of his own body. He found that he could move both arms but that his left hand hurt badly. It may be a broken bone or a bad sprain. His left leg hurt badly, but his right leg seemed OK. He evidently had burns all over his body as touching almost anywhere brought the pain.

He then tried to remain very still as he sensed that he may be in severe trouble? After all, it was very quiet? Why did he not hear any noise? Where were the helicopters that were always circling any LZ when an extraction was being executed? How long had he been knocked out? Where was everyone else?

All of these questions were streaming through his mind at once. He should be able to hear helicopters, rescue forces, and soldiers. He did not hear any of those things. It was at that moment he suddenly became very frightened. Fear was a tremendous motivator and for a few seconds, he had no pain whatsoever.

He tried to get up and found that he could not get his body to listen to his mental directives. He lay back down in the wet grass and decided he should rest until he could better see just what was around him, as he might be lying on or near something dangerous and would not even know it because of the darkness all around him. It would not be until daylight that he could take a realistic inventory of his condition.

He felt around his waist and was extremely thankful when he felt his 45-caliber pistol still attached on his belt. At least he had something to protect his life if required. He then took inventory of his entire combat web belt, which usually held grenades as well as his pistol. He could feel no grenades attached to his belt.

He also could not find his flashlight, which was usually attached to his combat vest where he could use it to read his map at night. The flashlight with its red lens was definitely missing, but he could still feel the map inside his shirt. He knew he still had his jungle boots on, but his right foot also hurt.

His tactical gloves were still on their clip hanging from his web harness. Since it was totally dark he could not see around him at all? But he sensed that he was lying in grass on the side of a hill, evidently off the actual LZ, which must be above him somewhere?

He spent the rest of the night on again, off again in states of semi-consciousness. He really was not completely sure how many hours he spent awake and how many hours he slept. He finally put his fingers to his mouth and discovered from the taste that the wetness on his face was definitely blood. The iron blood taste was unmistakable. He then began worrying if he might be bleeding to death.

He tried to examine his body again, but his position and pain kept him from doing very much to explore for any serious wounds. He would have to wait for daylight to really assess his condition and location. He just hoped that no enemy soldiers were looking for him, but then he realized that he heard no noise at all.

He just had to hope that he was not mortally wounded and hope that the army would come to his rescue soon and before the enemy found him wherever he was at the moment. He knew the army did not leave soldiers behind and that his unit would come to search for him when they determined what had happened to his platoon.

He then began to wonder about his RTO, Tim, and the other soldiers who had been standing beside him when the attack began. He thought that he had been holding the radio handset, so he knew that Corporal Turner, his RTO, should also be lying close to him now. But he heard no noise and he seemed to be totally alone.

A terrible sadness engulfed his mind. They had obviously been attacked while trying to leave the area. That meant that this was his fault! After all, he was the leader! He should have been more careful and perhaps he should have used his artillery targets on the adjacent hilltops before allowing the helicopters to come into the LZ? He had always been so careful to anticipate any and all dangers. Why had he missed the signals that the enemy was following or shadowing his platoon?

He then thought about his wife, Faith, who was presently assigned as an army nurse in the hospital at Camp Eagle, which was co-located with the 1/327th Battalion Rear Detachment near Phu Bai, Vietnam. She had volunteered to be an army nurse, just so she could serve her country, and also to be much closer to her husband Duke, as he served his combat tour in Vietnam.

She had told him in a letter that she did not want to stay alone in their quarters at Fort Benning for the entire year as he served his combat tour. She had joined the Army Nurse Corps and now was in Vietnam near him and he had just had his in country R&R with her just last month.

Did she know that his platoon had been attacked? How long would it be before someone told her of this combat action? He had updated his 'Next of Kin' forms last October when he knew she was signing an army contract for a six-month tour in Vietnam as a nurse. Faith was a very strong young woman and would not be deterred from serving her country alongside her infantry husband. They had both been raised in Texas to very strong parents and both felt a need to serve their country.

Duke had been raised on a ranch near Odessa, Texas, and knew that he would eventually serve his country in the military from the age of ten. Faith had been a tomboy in her teenage years and likewise wanted to serve her country in some capacity. They had met in High School briefly, but it was not until they were in their graduation year of college that they would become true lovers and soul mates forever.

Duke then thought about crying out for Corporal Turner, his RTO, but then thought better of the idea, as it might bring the wrong kind of rescue force, the North Vietnamese Army (NVA). If Corporal Turner was nearby, he would certainly know in the morning and they could then formulate their next moves.

He would just have to wait for the rescue force that would undoubtedly come at daylight. He knew the platoon extraction had been planned for just before dusk, in an attempt to fool the enemy as to where they were going next. That probably meant that there was little time for his commander to form a rescue force until the next morning.

But then he wondered again just how long he had been unconscious? Could he have slept through the rescue force arrival and departure? That would explain why he was here alone and why Corporal Turner was not here with him? Corporal Turner may have already been rescued. Perhaps they thought they had rescued all the live soldiers, and therefore thought he was already dead or among the burned bodies.

He felt around his waist again and found his canteen and slowly and quietly tried to free it from its cover so he could take a drink of water. He was so very thirsty. He finally managed to free the canteen only to discover that it had two holes in it and was half empty. He managed to get a couple of mouthfuls of water before it all leaked out.

Could things get any worse? Hell yes, they could. He could yet be discovered by the enemy and then immediately killed or captured. He had to remain silent until he could better access his condition and location. He might yet have to change gears and go into escape and evasion mode.

His next thoughts were once again of his wife, Faith, and the Double Star Ranch in Texas. Would he live to see them both again? It was not looking real good right now, that's for sure. What would Faith do if he died in the Republic of Vietnam? Would Faith marry again, have a family and remember him? He had to stop this, as he was now torturing himself.

He was in and out of consciousness over the next two hours. He was in his dreams back in High School as the Quarterback of his high school football team. They were behind in score by only 3 points and it was up to him to pull out the win. He tried every play he knew to no avail. The team was just not getting any breaks and the referees had already made two tough calls against his team.

They were now three yards from a first down and he only had one more chance to make the yardage or they would most likely lose the ball and then the game by just three points.

He took the team into the huddle and then called for the one trick play that they had left. It was a double reverse with the ball coming back to him to pass a 'Hail Mary' to his best running back. It was a long shot, but he knew the opposing team would not see it coming as they thought he was going on the ground for the three yards. He then noticed that the running back he was speaking to was actually Corporal Tim Turner, his RTO. How could that be?

The play started and the double reverse worked perfectly and the ball was back in Duke's hands in just seconds, while the opposing team members were chasing down players on both sides of the formation. Duke pulled out of the pocket and fell back and gave the ball all he had in a throw toward Tim Turner heading toward the end zone. Everything came together and it worked perfectly as Tim hauled in the ball and crossed the goal line. The crowd erupted into a thunderous roar as everyone ran to the end zone.

It was the win of his lifetime. He was the star of the entire High School for the next week. Then reality returned and he woke up cold and sweating at the same time. What a wild dream? The win of his dreams was now gone and the loss of his lifetime was starring him in the face here in the darkness. He was alone, a loser among losers, and he had failed his platoon. He felt terrible. This was entirely his fault.

His mind was ramped up. His nervous system was obviously working on adrenaline and fear, injury, and the repercussions of his situation were ruling over his ability to even think clearly. He then heard his first noise and it was not reassuring. He heard some animal above him growling. Evidently, some animal had smelled blood and was now planning an attack. As if things could not get any worse?

He knew he could not use his 45caliber pistol, except as a last resort, as the sound of the shot would inevitably bring the enemy to his location. He knew the enemy was close since they had already attacked his platoon. He would have to use a knife or his bare hands.

He felt again around his belt looking for the Buck knife that he always carried. Thank God it was still there. He tried to turn slightly to pull out the knife and at that moment he slid slightly and felt thin air off to his left as he reached out. He continued to reach his hand out for more ground and found none. It was at that moment that he realized he was evidently on some kind of ledge, high in the air with nothing but air and a huge fall just off to his left.

My God, no wonder no one had found him here, he was evidently hanging off the side of the LZ. He had to stay awake now, as falling back asleep could be fatal if he rolled and fell off this ledge. He now also knew why he could hear the animal above and why the animal had not yet attacked? The animal was likewise surprised about his location and evidently could not easily get to him. It must be a predator pacing back and forth on the LZ hoping to get at the prey he could smell below?

He was on a rock and grass ledge. He immediately thought back to his earlier life, when he had to recite bible verses in church. His assignment had been Psalm 40, and he now remembered that Psalm clearly:

"I waited patiently for the Lord;
he turned to me and heard my cry,
he lifted me out of the slimy pit,
out of the mud and the mire;
he set my feet on a rock,
and gave me a firm place to stand.
May all who want to take my life,
be put to shame and confusion,
may all who desire my ruin,
be turned back in disgrace."

The passage was all about being saved by the lord, and learning that the righteous would win over evil. The fact that the verse had come back to him warmed his heart. God had saved him just as the psalm had promised. His enemies, be they animals or NVA, could not touch him at the moment.

God had intervened in his life. It was an absolutely awesome thought. He would have to send up a prayer of thanks to the Lord. He had not been praying lately, and he knew at that moment that he would have to change his ways, and fast! He thanked God for his intervention as he then fell back into a semiconscious state.

The time seemed to drag on incredibly slowly. His senses were much more aware now of his surroundings and he could hear an assortment of jungle sounds all around him. Why had he never heard most of these noises before? Obviously, these sounds were part of the jungle every night but they seemed so much more ominous now. He then knew the answers to his own questions. He had never really heard the jungle sounds before because he had never been alone out here before.

He had never had to worry about any animal sounds before. He had always felt very secure with his platoon of soldiers in a perimeter around him. He knew the routine sounds of an approaching enemy, but the critters of the jungle did not seem to bother him before. Now, everything and anything could be a potential threat.

He now imagined every kind of predator; animal, snake, and spider were all approaching him at this very minute. He knew his mind was playing tricks on him, but he felt helpless to prevent his own worst fears. He looked around again as his eyes began to focus a bit better. As dawn approached, he could now see things that he had not noticed before.

He was definitely on a ledge above a huge valley below. He looked up and could not make out the top of the hill or just how far down this hill he was presently located. He could now also see a little to his left and right and could see no other soldiers or equipment on the ledge with him.

He once again wondered about his RTO, Corporal Turner. They had been side by side on the LZ above, so surely he was nearby? Then again, perhaps only Duke had been thrown clear of the LZ and Corporal Turner had been blown apart by one of the mortar rounds or wounded and requiring help on the LZ above? The thought of Tim's possible demise was very distressful to Duke. The young man was his favorite member of his platoon. He had hand-selected the boy to be his RTO.

Tim was quiet, always sat alone as if he had a terrible secret that he did not want to be known by the others. He was smart and showed intelligence in everything he did. The Platoon Sergeant had used Tim several times to do various chores that Duke knew were important to SFC Bell. SFC Bell would not have chosen the young soldier unless he trusted him implicitly. Therefore, Duke acted on his own basic instincts and selected Tim as his RTO. He had never been sorry with his decision.

Duke had found out that the lad had joined the army immediately before his eighteenth birthday. That fact alone told Duke that either Tim wanted to get out of a bad situation at home or that Tim had a goal for himself. He also liked the boy's spunk and drive. Tim reminded Duke of Jimmy Brown from the old football team, a guy Duke could always rely on. Tim learned quickly and was always ready to volunteer for anything that Duke needed.

Duke had selected him early on to be his RTO. The RTO of the Platoon was a very special position. The RTO and the Lieutenant were inseparable daily. Tim knew he had to stay no more than one arm's length from his LT. The radio was the platoon's lifeline to fire support and the LT was the source of instructions that could save the platoon in any contact. Tim Turner quickly became the sidekick, bodyguard, and Aide-de-camp to Lieutenant Duke Gabriel. They were a good team.

Duke wondered once again where Tim was. It was not like Tim to have left Duke alone. That meant that Tim must be dead, a thought that very much distressed the young lieutenant. Duke tried to stay awake through all of these thoughts, but his fatigue finally got the best of him and he fell back asleep, wet, cold, scared, and alone.

Chapter Four: Graduation Day 1968

19 Months Earlier

Faith Anderson and Duke Gabriel

Today was a very special day for Faith Anderson. She was graduating fifth in her class at The University of Texas Nursing School in record time since she had attended school every summer cutting off one full year of the program. Her parents and two of her siblings had come down to Austin, Texas, from San Angelo with several of her extended relatives to see her graduate from the nursing program.

It was the seventh of June 1968 and she was sitting eight rows back in the audience as the various schools and majors were being directed to the stage for their diplomas. The University Quad was packed with parents, friends, and relatives of all of the graduating seniors.

The University of Texas actually had several graduation ceremonies every June, depending on your major and the availability of the University Quad where these ceremonies were conducted outside if the weather permitted. It just so happened that her nursing school was currently sharing space on the Quad with the University's ROTC Department and its Army and Air

Force Commissioning Ceremony for the ROTC graduating seniors.

The new lieutenants had already graduated from the University of Texas the day before in the General Graduation Ceremony, which had been much larger and had been held indoors because of rain yesterday. Now the new Army and Air Force lieutenants were in uniform and waiting for their 'pinning on ceremony' of their new gold second lieutenant bars.

Faith was talking quietly with a friend to her right when something flashed in the rows ahead of her, which drew her attention away from her friend. It was the sun gleaming off the new lieutenant bars of a young man moving toward the stage to receive his official Army Commissioning certificate. Faith had seen the young man before, back in high school over four years earlier and just recently at the beach during spring break on Padre Island. They had actually dated one or two times. But his new mature appearance drew her in like a magnet.

His stride was natural and very graceful for a man. He moved absolutely effortlessly as if he had no cares in the world whatsoever. It was the stride of complete and utter confidence. His face was clean-shaven and his hair cut short, but not the crew cut of many of the others in the line. He still had the very distinctive look of a Texas cowboy. It was Adam Duke Gabriel.

Faith zeroed in on the young man. She had always liked what she saw in Duke Gabriel and elbowed her friend gently saying, "That's Duke Gabriel from the Double Star Ranch at the top of the stairs leading to the stage right there?" Her friend, Julie Bennett, looked at the stage and said quietly, "I don't know him, but I get first dibs if he turns you down. He's a doll!

Faith laughed and said she had no intention of approaching him, but that she had dated him a couple of times in high school which seemed like years ago. She managed to say out loud to Julie that, "I do like the cut of his uniform." Julie smiled and said, "Yeah, just the cut of his uniform eh? What about those shoulders and that cute little butt too?"

Faith giggled and said that she had to admit that she liked the looks of the entire package, but he was probably either married by now or played the field with looks like that. Both girls giggled so loudly that the young man actually turned his head and looked their way. Faith then wanted to crawl and hide under her chair.

Army Second Lieutenant Adam Duke Gabriel heard the 'giggling' in the audience and raised his head to see where it was coming from. He saw two girls about seven rows back, but they were just a bit far away to see distinct features, but one was definitely a very pretty blond. Then, the hair on his arms suddenly rose up.

That reaction almost never happened unless there was a danger present or something unexplained had just caught his complete attention. He really could not explain the physical response, except that he had first noticed such a reaction while hunting as a boy with his father many years ago. It was part of his body's early warning system.

The hair lifting on his arms often was a sign that something unusual was about to happen. It was a signal that he never ignored. His entire body came to alert, all senses searching for 'something' unknown.

The ceremony continued and Duke Gabriel got his commissioning certificate and went back to his seat in the second row. Something was bothering him, but he did not know what it was. There was something in the air, some unknown force that had just manifested itself while he was on the stage. He looked around his seat. He did not know what he was looking for exactly, but he thought he would know it when he saw it.

His friend Brent Cross asked him what was bothering him? Duke looked at Brent and said, "You would not believe me if I told you." Brent then said, "You look like something unexpected is about to happen?" Duke just shrugged and said, "Not unexpected really, but surely unlikely or unusual." Brent went back to reading his program. He was used to 'The Duke' saying unusual things. His friend Adam Gabriel could be rather deep at times.

Adam could not pinpoint his feelings but he knew that something had just happened. He just wondered if he would ever know just what it was. The rest of the ceremony was uneventful. After the ceremony, Duke went to supper with his brother and parents at a local restaurant. Duke was now a newly minted officer in the United States Army and would soon be headed for Fort Benning to attend officer training school and then the Army's Ranger School.

Faith Anderson likewise went to supper with her family. They decided to go to the new lobster and seafood restaurant that had just opened the past winter in Austin, Texas. Everyone loved the restaurant and the prices were not too high, so her father loved the place. Her younger brother, Alex, could probably eat endless shrimp until the place would go bankrupt! Alex's stomach was almost a bottomless pit since he had turned sixteen just last month.

The waitress brought their seafood dinners and Faith was enjoying her fried shrimp basket with hot French Fries when a party of four passed their large table headed for a booth in the corner of the restaurant. It was Adam Duke Gabriel and his family. Faith's eyes automatically followed the young man in uniform as he walked between the tables. Duke once again had one of his funny feelings and began to look around the restaurant. His eyes locked with Faith's and Duke then tripped over his own feet and almost went down on the floor.

Duke stabilized himself while continuing to walk and look at Faith Anderson, and then he slid into the booth directly across from the Anderson's table. Duke was mesmerized. He was looking at the most beautiful woman he had ever seen. The hair on his arms was once again standing and he felt chills run up his back. His father asked him if everything was OK, and Duke replied, "I'm fine dad, just tripped a little, that's all." But he never took his eyes off the blond beauty sitting across the way.

Faith tore her eyes away from Duke and stumbled back into the conversation at their table. But she kept sneaking looks at Duke when she thought she could get away with it. On one such quick look, she locked eyes once again with Duke, and Duke lit up in a smile that absolutely stole her heart away with its brilliance.

Duke could not believe what he was looking at. He had never before had such a reaction to any young woman. He tried to tell himself that she was just a pretty face and that was all, but his senses told him otherwise. He felt he knew her somehow, but could not quite place the time or location of their previous meeting. He just had to know who she was and where she lived.

Duke ordered his meal and talked with his parents and younger brother until their orders were delivered to the table. Meanwhile, the Andersons completed their meal and got up to leave. Duke quickly excused himself leaving his supper to get cold and followed the Andersons out of the main restaurant and into the restaurant lobby.

By this time, Duke had remembered seeing her giggling with another girl at the earlier graduation ceremony and was sure she was a classmate he had never met. He awkwardly moved up next to Faith in the lobby of the restaurant and said, “Hi, I’m Duke Gabriel, and I believe we are classmates, as I saw you at the graduation ceremony earlier today.” Faith replied, “Yes, I just graduated from the School of Nursing.”

Duke said that he had also just graduated from UT and was just commissioned in the Army. Faith then looked him up and down and said, “Yes, I figured that since you are still in uniform.” Duke looked down a bit foolishly at himself and said, “Yea, I guess you would figure that out pretty easily, eh?” They both laughed and then Faith said, “ You look good in it, and just for the record you and I have met before.”

Duke gave her his best “Aw Shucks” Texas cowboy smile and then asked her where they had met before. Faith told him that they had actually dated a couple of times in high school and that she was Faith Anderson from San Angelo High School. Duke was dumbfounded. He did remember dating a Faith Anderson, but that girl looked nothing like this raving beauty standing in front of him. That girl had been a gawkily skinny tomboy!

He stumbled through the next several words, saying something about how she had aged well. She laughed and told him that he did not look too bad himself. Duke asked her if she might like meeting him for coffee or a movie again sometime? She said yes, and they exchanged phone numbers and hotel information. Duke then excused himself, said goodbye, and headed back to his parents' table. Faith's mother leaned over to Faith and said, "Do you know that young man? Do you really think you should be going out with a complete stranger?"

Faith smiled and said, "He's an Army Officer mother, not a serial killer, and he is not a complete stranger. I actually dated him in high school once or twice." Faith liked what she had seen in Duke. He seemed much more real to her than her memories of him, which was much more than she had seen in any other young man lately. She silently hoped that he would call.

That evening Faith did some quiet background checks and more research about Adam Duke Gabriel? She called several friends to ask questions about him. She found out that he had become a serious young man and had not dated too much in college. Faith liked serious young men and decided that this new 'Duke' was possibly worth giving some time to. Now she just had to wait until he called.

She accompanied her family out to the cars where everyone said their goodbyes and all headed for the various hotels they were staying in Austin for the weekend.

Chapter Five: Day Two Alone In the Vietnam Jungle

April 1970

Duke woke up to bright sun bearing down on his body and a light sheen of sweat over his face. He could now see just where he was, and it was not a comforting scene. He estimated that it must be close to noon, because the sun was almost directly overhead. He was lying in a foliage-covered ditch off the side of a hilltop with pretty steep downward slopes on all sides of his position but up. He had difficulty looking upward as the heavy foliage almost completely covered his body.

He once again sent up a silent prayer to God for allowing him to land on this stone ledge and live. He felt that had to be a sign that he was meant to survive. Now he just had to figure out what to do next!

He then looked out over one of the most spectacular views that he had ever seen in Vietnam. Hanging off the side of this mountain had given him a view of the entire Ashau Valley further to the west and a lowland valley heading east. Because he was almost always in the thick canopy jungle, he had never really had an opportunity to see such a spectacular view of the entire area that he now saw directly in front of him. He could literally see for miles from this position.

He had been blown off the hilltop above and by the 'Grace of God,' he had landed in the only available place on the side of the hill that could possibly have stopped his fall for over 200 feet further below. It was a long flat ledge that appeared to wrap around this side of the hilltop that was probably not even visible from the hill above his location.

Good God, how was he going to get out of this position? He would probably need climbing gear and rope and he obviously did not have either! He spent the next hour moving slightly in every direction to try and sit upright and get a true sense of just where he was located.

He took out his map and immediately saw the picture of his wife Faith he had clipped to his map that was always close to his heart inside his shirt. The picture was still there attached to the map. Thank God the picture had not been lost in the explosions on the LZ. He was so glad that they had married each other the previous year, as he now had to wonder if he would ever see her again. He then began to study the elevation lines on the tactical map. Yep, Hill 786 was, in fact, an outcropping to the mountain to which the hill and LZ were attached.

He had not noticed that before when he was making his plans for extraction. It was kind of like thinking the world was flat when you could only see in two directions, forward and upward. When you really studied the map and factored in the elevation indicators, you could clearly see that the LZ was sitting on a separate outcropping jutting out from the overall mountain. But of course, none of those perceptions helped him now.

He finally decided that he was in fact, still pretty much intact, and had all four limbs and all ten fingers and still had both arms and both legs. That alone was a great relief. But he hurt all over and even some of his internal organs seemed to be screaming in pain. Both of his kidneys hurt, and he had to pee something awful, and every muscle in his body hurt. Obviously being blown off the LZ by the explosions left his body in a real hurt!

He decided to just lie there for a few more minutes and to once again take a personal inventory of his body and surroundings. The blood on the side of his face had dried into a large scab that appeared to start in his left hairline and ran down the left side of his face. His lips were split in several places and his chin had a large cut. His teeth hurt, and he could feel at least two of them were loose in his lower jaw. He was finally able to open the fly in his jungle fatigues and managed to relieve himself over the ledge. Thank God he still had that piece of male equipment also!

He then did another quick scan of his body in the strong light of day. Unbelievably, he found no bullet or shrapnel holes in his torso, arms, or legs. There was a C-ration can lying next to his leg and his first instinct was to kick it off the ledge to listen to it fall. He immediately regretted his decision, as he was going to need to eat something, and he had just kicked a potential meal off the ledge.

He heard it hit the ground below after a long fall. How perfectly stupid! His left knee hurt very badly and he wondered if it might be broken. He tried to flex the knee and it protested badly. Perhaps it was not broken as he could flex the leg, but then again, he had not tried to put any weight on it yet?

His next thoughts turned to the army and his platoon, company, and battalion. Surely his company commander would come looking for him? And where was his RTO? He remembered that they had been standing next to each other when Duke pushed Corporal Turner to the ground during the explosions. So Corporal Turner should be close to where Duke now lay. He remembered clearly pushing Corporal Turner to the ground when the hair on Duke's arm had risen up.

He looked down off the side of the hill to see if he could see anyone at the bottom of the hill, but the jungle greenery prevented any view of the bottom of the hill. If Corporal Tim Turner had been thrown over this ledge, there would be nothing to stop his body from slamming into the bottom some 200 feet below. A fall like that would certainly have been fatal. He felt bad for Corporal Turner, as he probably never knew what had killed him.

He lay there just thinking for the next hour. By looking at the sun above Duke figured he probably had about six or seven more hours of daylight left. What was his best move at this point? Could the enemy be up on top of the hill? Should he try to move and climb back up the hill? All of these thoughts brought more complications.

If the enemy had moved onto the LZ after his platoon had left, he could be walking or crawling himself right into a prison or worse. He had not heard any more helicopters, so it was unlikely that any American soldiers were on the LZ above his location. But he also did not hear any movement above that might signal that the enemy was on the LZ.

Why hadn't his company commander come back to the LZ to get him? The answer to that question had to be relatively simple. They thought he was dead! No American unit ever left wounded soldiers behind. It just was not done. If they thought that Duke was alive, or even if they thought he was dead, they would have come back to get his body.

That had to mean that the army believed they had retrieved all of the bodies or survivors. He had been knocked unconscious, so perhaps the army had come back looking for him, found and rescued Corporal Turner, but did not see him lying here in this ditch? If the bodies had been badly burned, Company D might not have identified and sorted out all of the bodies yet?

The mortar explosions had been extremely accurate and Duke had never seen so many mortar rounds hit in such a small area all at once before. The enemy must have used several mortar tubes all firing at once. There was absolutely no escape from the terrible onslaught of explosions as they had hit the LZ. He still was unsure exactly just what had happened. One minute he was directing his soldiers onto the birds, and the next moment he was on the ground and everything and everybody was in a flaming inferno.

The enemy must have been lying in wait for the helicopters. They had held their fire until the last set of birds had landed knowing that the army would not even know there had been an attack while the enemy soldiers had plenty of time to leave the area. That could possibly have prevented the US Army to effectively launch a counterattack.

It was an extremely well executed mortar ambush. He kicked himself again for not being prepared for such an ambush. It had never happened to him before and he had allowed his guard to slide. Once again he thought this attack was his entire fault! He had been completely unprepared and his failure had cost lives in his platoon.

He kicked himself for not doing more to prevent such an attack. He should have called artillery onto all of the surrounding hilltops before he called for the helicopters, thereby possibly hitting the mortar squad while they were setting up their tubes. But he had no warning whatsoever of their close proximity to his platoon. They had not seen any enemy soldiers in this area for the past two weeks. That's why they were leaving the area. Hindsight did not change the current situation. He was now trapped on a thin ledge and evidently all alone.

He decided to lie there a while just to make sure that he did not hear any noise or activity up the hill on the LZ. During that time, he took inventory once again of his body, its hurts, and signals of injuries. He decided to crawl to each side of the ledge to see if he could find a possible way to climb upward. He crawled to his left a few feet to where he found a small natural indentation that might give him some traction and a more natural route where he might be able to crawl back up to the LZ using only his hands and feet.

Duke finally decided that he had been lying there procrastinating long enough. He felt he had to use the available daylight and he had to try to climb upward. He started to claw his way up the hill in the small indentation he had just found that looked like it might just go all the way up to the top of the hill. It was very slow going as the hill was steep and his body hurt everywhere.

It was while trying to climb up the hill to the LZ that he first heard the slight noise further to his right. He stopped immediately and listened hard. Good God, there was someone up on the LZ! It could be anyone? But he knew that if the battalion were there looking for him that they would probably make a lot more noise, and he would have heard helicopters and he had not heard any such noise in the last hour.

So what had he just heard? It sounded familiar, like a human voice. He froze perfectly still and listened intently. There! He heard it again! It was movement, not a voice, and it was closer to him than he first recognized. He immediately looked right and left in search of the noise that was now echoing over the valley below.

He immediately turned and began to explore further around the corner to his right on the ledge. It was then that he rounded the corner and found Corporal Turner. He appeared badly wounded, with one leg twisted under his body in such a way that it had to be completely broken. He had burns on his face, arms, and legs and probably looked a lot like Duke, himself.

Tim's cheek and mouth had been severely cut and he was unable to communicate at all. His eyes were as big as saucers, he was crying, and when he saw Duke he tried in vain to smile. But the smile reminded Duke of a Halloween pumpkin face twisted sideways. He was a real mess of human flesh and bone. He looked like he was close to death.

Duke crawled over the to the young soldier and began to look him over from head to foot. Miraculously, he too had no bullet holes or severe wounds except for readily apparent cuts, burns, and breaks. But it became very obvious quickly and completely that he would be unable to crawl or walk and this became the first real logistical problem for Lieutenant Duke Gabriel.

The ledge was wider here where Corporal Turner had landed and Duke would have to try and make the young soldier comfortable and begin planning how to get him off this ledge. He thought to himself, "What more could the Lord throw at him today?" The Lord was certainly testing his young lieutenant today!

He immediately saw that Corporal Turner still had his canteen attached to his web belt and he retrieved the canteen and gave the Corporal small drinks of water for the next several minutes. It was obvious that Tim was in great pain and Duke knew that he had to find one of the platoon's first aid kits which all routinely contained multiple morphine injectors.

He leaned close and told Corporal Turner to "hold on", that he was going to go for help or see what he could get to make Corporal Turner more comfortable. He told Turner to keep quiet as they were abandoned here in the jungle and the enemy might be close, and Duke did not want the enemy to discover their location.

Corporal Turner acknowledged the LT's words but then grabbed his arm mumbling as best he could, "Please don't leave me here". Duke held the young man's hand and leaned in close and said, "Don't you worry Tim, I will never leave you alone." Turner just smiled and laid his head back against the rock.

Duke told him that he had to recon the hill to see it was safe for both of them to go up to the LZ and that he had to find a first aid kit if possible. Duke then began clawing his way to the top of the hill. It took him almost an hour to get back up to the LZ. It was already late afternoon now and he had little time before dusk.

He hurriedly took inventory of the items lying on the abandoned LZ. He found Corporal Turner's rucksack and radio and several other rucksacks, but was not able to find his own? He tried to turn the radio on but it would not function. But he knew that Turner carried their first aid kit. So he grabbed Turner's rucksack, got the first aid kit and then quickly hid the rucksack in the thick brush off to the side of the LZ.

He did likewise with four other rucksacks that were still lying on the LZ. He just wanted to put them out of sight, as he would need to come back and take a complete inventory when he had more time. They all had contained C-rations, which he and Tim would need later and he did not want to take them down to Turner and then have to carry them back up again later.

Duke set to work immediately hiding anything and everything that might prove valuable later for their survival. He tried to hide everything he had found on the LZ in the thick brush well away from the LZ. He had found several first aid kits, an entrenching tool (folding shovel), some loose ammunition, and several loose grenades. The small arms ammunition would be of little use, as he could not find any M-16's that would use the ammo. Clearly, someone had returned and took all the small arms weapons with them when they left.

They probably would have taken the grenades too, but they had been hidden under several C-rations in one of the rucksacks. Clearly one of his soldiers had thought he wanted to carry more grenades than he was allowed, and had hidden them under his food. Duke thought he would have to chastise the young man, and then he thought, "My God, the kid is probably dead!

Carrying loose grenades under canned C-rations in a rucksack was strongly discouraged and exceedingly dangerous, as any pin could jostle out of any one grenade and you could literally blow your own ass off!

He then emptied two more of the rucksacks out and put all of the grenades into a hole he had hastily dug using the little shovel, covered over the contents with debris and leaves and then loaded one of the empty rucksacks with two first aid kits and two C-rations from the stash for he and Tim to eat tonight down on the ledge.

He had also found the light nylon rope that the platoon often used to save pilots from their parachutes when they were caught in trees after baling out of their aircraft. The "Rescue Rope' was always carried by his fourth squad. He would need the rope tomorrow morning to help pull Tim up the steep hill. He slung the rope around his body like a lumberjack. He then started to walk off the LZ and stepped into a small pothole and heard his knee crack and he went down.

He knew his knee had been damaged but he had hoped it was just ligament damage like he had experienced before in high school while playing football. But now he knew that he had probably just broken his kneecap or knee, as the pain was extreme. He must have had a hairline fracture or small break and the pothole was enough to do the rest.

He hobbled the rest of the way off the LZ on hill 786 and into the jungle to hide the rest of the booty he had managed to find that might be of use for survival later. He did not hide the 'Rescue Rope' as he wanted to take it with him back down to Tim. They would need that rope tomorrow to bring Tim up here and Tim was in no condition to catch the rope if he tried to throw it down from the LZ tomorrow.

But right now, Duke was in no shape to do much more at all. He had to get back down to Tim with food and water before it got dark again and then they would both take some morphine from the first aid kits to help stem their terrible pain.

Finally he managed to cut several short branches using his buck knife that he would need to reinforce his own knee and in order to splint Tim's leg. He chose small green branches for his own knee that might still allow him some movement and much stronger straight branches to use on Tim's leg.

He then made his way back to the edge of the LZ, looked and listened for any sounds of movement once again, and then began to slide back down the hill to the ledge where Corporal Turner still lay badly wounded and badly broken. He had to move very slowly as he was trying to slide down the hill while holding the branches he had cut and with the rope around his neck and a rucksack on his back.

He had contemplated tying the rope to a tree off the side of the LZ, but decided not too, as it could alert the enemy that they were below, if the enemy came to the LZ before they could escape the ledge. Dusk was approaching fast, and he needed to get back to the ledge while he could still see and try to administer to Corporal Turner's wounds and needs.

Once back to Tim's location, he opened the first aid kits, found the combat morphine and immediately stuck a morphine injector into Tim's thigh and then another shot into his own thigh. He then took the two cans of rations out of his rucksack and he opened the cans and fed one to Corporal Turner. The Corporal was visibly upset with this action.

Corporal Turner knew that he was supposed to help the LT, not the other way around, and he was clearly very upset at the reversal of roles. Tears rolled down his face as he thanked his LT for coming back to him. He then very slowly managed to tell the LT that he did not want to die on this ledge alone.

Duke once again told the young Corporal that they were in this situation together and he would not abandon his RTO. He also told Tim that he was not going to die here. After all, Tim was with the Ranger, and the Ranger would get him out of here! Tim managed to smile just a little as the morphine took effect.

Chapter Six: Adam 'Duke" Gabriel
(Two Years Earlier)
Graduation Day, 1968

Adam Duke Gabriel was born in Killeen, Texas, in May of 1946. His father and mother were second-generation cattle ranchers; he and his brother would be the third generation. His family owned a Texas cattle ranch named The Double Star, which was actually located further west and south of Odessa, Texas. Adam had been born in Killen while his parents were living there, because his father was serving in the Army in 1946 at Fort Hood, Texas, at the time.

The Double Star was named after the only two "stars" that could be seen clearly from the property when Duke's grandfather had bought the property. He had no idea what the stars were named, but it was enough that he had seen two stars early that first night and so he named the ranch the 'Double Star', which was easy to make into a very distinctive branding iron for the cattle. The two smaller stars were contained inside the famous Texas Star logo to make a great Branding Iron for the ranch.

Duke loved ranching and planned to return to the family business once he got his college degree in business and agricultural husbandry and once he had served his country. The University of Texas gave him the opportunity to be both close to home and get the education he would need to run the ranch when his father stepped aside.

Ranching was becoming more and more scientific in nature, and now required book keeping and financial business skills. The family ranch had steadily grown into a moderately large operation with over sixty cowboys at one time or another during the year. They raised and bred longhorn cattle and quarter horses and were known throughout Texas as a good-sized family operation.

Duke grew up under a cowboy hat and even had his own custom style boots made almost every year since age twelve to keep up with his fast growth. He loved tall dark brown leather boots with a custom heal that allowed him good footing while both walking and when in the saddle. All of his handmade boots had the words, 'The Duke', stitched somewhere on the shaft of the boot. It was his form of a trademark so to speak. His 'John Wayne' namesake was never far from his mind and he intended to live up to the famous name his father had bestowed upon him.

He worked at the ranch all of his life through high school and spent almost every summer on the ranch moving cattle from pasture to pasture and having a permanent tan line on the back of his neck. Even in college, he spent his holidays and summers at the ranch and that's probably why he had rarely crossed paths with Miss. Faith Anderson, the woman who would become his own shining star later in life.

Duke played sports all through high school and excelled in both football and track. While he played both positions of quarterback and wide receiver from time to time, he was a star nonetheless at catching almost anything ever thrown to him. In either position, if he had the ball and started running, it seemed that no one could run him down before he crossed the goal line.

Because of his stunning good looks and athletic build, young women had constantly pursued him. He dated in high school, but he was rather immature at the time and no one ever seemed to impress him or rise to the level of his mother. He had met Faith Anderson at several high school football games, but at the time, Duke was not interested in much else except football. He never really got to know Faith Anderson except for a passing interest in rather obscure social gatherings when the schools played football against one another.

Girls were just not his main interest in his early years. Not that he was a Momma's boy, but he deeply respected his mother and eventually wanted a partner like his father had married. He wanted a girl that talked about more than the latest craze, fad, and music.

By the time he got to college, he had matured considerably and Duke wanted a serious partner for the rest of his life. But a serious minded woman who actually wanted to live on a working cattle ranch appeared to be a difficult thing to find in college. So he had decided to wait until he met that 'special someone' to begin getting serious.

Duke was a truly multifaceted person. He was tough, yet sensitive. He was good-looking but not egotistical. He was religious, but not an evangelist. But most of all, he was realistic. He knew that some people of both sexes liked to manipulate others. He had seen this at work in many relationships he had witnessed throughout high school and college. He, therefore, was probably more skeptical about dating the opposite sex than most of his college contemporaries.

He wanted a spouse that was multi-dimensional. He wanted a true partner, not just someone who wanted a free ride. Ranching was a tough life. He needed a wife and equal partner that was willing to work beside him in the many tasks that had to be accomplished every day on a ranch. But he also wanted someone sensitive and loving. His mother and father had the perfect chemistry and combination needed to make a working ranch successful. He wanted the same perfect match.

Such a partner in life had to be realistic, hardworking, supportive, and willing to take on a challenge in life. He wanted no wallflower or weeping willow. That's why his mother was such a tremendous force in his perception of the life mate necessary to run a ranching operation. That meant searching the field of available women for someone with a beautiful strong character. Of course, she must also be attractive. He wanted someone that he could be proud to have on his arm. It was his one concession to vanity.

That's why after the age of twenty-one, he was constantly scanning the horizon of life looking for some unknown waiting woman. He even laughed many times about his search to his friend Brent Cross, who thought his search was unrealistic. Brent subscribed to the theory that you just had to have some sexual chemistry with a woman, and the rest would work itself out.

Duke did not believe that at all. Believing that you could change anyone was a false premise in Duke's world. He had to find just the right woman, a woman that not only loved him but someone who would be a true partner and not just an ornament on his arm.

That's precisely why he was so interested when he saw Faith Anderson in the crowd at graduation and later again on the same day at the seafood restaurant. His body even had a visceral reaction to her very presence. Duke believed in 'Fate' or "God's plans" for your life. God appeared to be putting Faith into Duke's line of vision a lot lately. That had to mean something?

He knew that a lot of women like Faith's friend Julie Bennett, seemed to exist in college only with the intent that they were there to find a spouse. Adam thought that such 'husband hunters' were not in college to seriously pursue a career or even necessarily to better themselves intellectually. Therefore he was cautiously optimistic, but rarely head over heals, over anyone thrown in front of him at any given time.

Duke believed that God had played a direct role in the picking of his name and that God had also played in his choice to serve his country and now he felt that God had also played a role for him to find this woman, Faith Anderson, not once, but twice in a single day. It was even more coincidental that this particular woman was someone that he had previously dated once or twice but at a time when he was too immature to see the real woman standing right in front of him. He felt he had to follow this silent signal to see if she might just be the woman that God was placing again and again in his path for a reason.

That's why he had gotten out of the family booth at the restaurant to follow her to the lobby. That's also why he approached her so brazenly, something he had never in his life done before. He had never walked up to a total stranger and asked for a date. It was not in his makeup to do such a thing. But his mind and body were screaming internally for him to do just that.

She even accepted his date proposal as if she had known him all of her life. Adam felt that it was a sign that he had done the right thing. After all, what's the worst that could happen? He might find out that they were completely incompatible and would lose the price of coffee. But, Oh, what if she turned out to be the 'One', the only woman in the world for Adam Gabriel?

He walked back to his table smiling both outwardly and internally. Faith had given him her parent's home phone number in San Angelo, and also told him she was staying with her parents at the local Hilton Hotel in Austin until Monday when she and her family would return to San Angelo.

Upon returning to his table, His father immediately asked, "What was that all about?" Duke then said, "Ah nothing at all, dad, just thought I had recognized someone, that's all." The family went back to eating and Duke now had much more on his plate than just cold food. His mind was spinning.

Once Duke and his family returned to their hotel, Duke changed out of his uniform and put on his jeans, western snap-button shirt, and boots. He always felt he could think clearer when he was dressed in his normal everyday attire. He soon managed to come up with an excuse to leave the hotel room for a few minutes to meet Brent Cross for a drink in the bar before everyone separated headed in their various directions. He did meet Brent for a quick drink, but then told Brent that he had to leave for a previous date.

He immediately took a taxicab to the Hilton Hotel in Austin in search of one Miss Faith Anderson. When he got to the hotel, he approached the front desk and asked to be put through to the Anderson room. Mrs. Alice Anderson answered the call and Duke asked for Faith. Faith came on the line and Duke then said, "This is Adam Duke Gabriel and I wondered if this was a good time to have that coffee I promised you? I'm in the lobby and they have a coffee shop right here." Faith said, "Well, Adam, you are nothing if not persistent." Duke said, "Well, my mother always told me that the early bird usually got the worm." I intend to be early!

Faith just laughed, and oh how good it sounded to Duke. Faith said that she would be down in a minute and asked him to grab a table and that she liked her coffee with milk or cream. Adam moved to the café, which was located, right off the lobby and obtained a table. He ordered two Coffee Lattes, and two slices of cinnamon coffee cake. By the time the coffees and cake reached the table, Faith had entered the front of the café. Duke stood and then held the chair out for Faith.

The next hour was spent in an amicable conversation between the two young adults as they found themselves each in the company of someone very compatible. They hit it off almost instantly. They found they liked the same things, liked the same music, and felt comfortable in each other's company. In fact, they enjoyed each other's company so much, that time flew as they sat huddled together over a very small table.

Their short date for coffee would start a relationship and love affair that would last for the next six decades. Faith and Duke both truly thought that the moment was very important in their respective lives. They were both now adults over the age of twenty-one and exchanged personal information, addresses, and phone numbers. Duke then invited Faith to his family's ranch for a visit this summer before they both started their respective lives and careers.

Faith said there was absolutely no way she could come to the ranch for very long because she had to work at her father's store and she also had a horse named Wildflower that she had to care for all summer. But she would talk with her parents about maybe coming for a short visit if they thought they could manage without her.

Duke told her that his family had a guest cabin on the ranch that was used for visitors and that her entire family could also come if it would make her parents feel more comfortable. He told her that they would all love the ranch. He also told her to bring her horse, as they had plenty of stalls and corals.

Faith told him that her mother and father would never be able to take much time off from their store or be away from their church very long and that she was currently considering joining the Army Reserve herself, as they had a special program for nurses. She said her siblings had summer jobs and likewise could not take time off for a long vacation.

Adam said that he had to report to the army at Fort Benning, Georgia on July 25, 1968, but that still gave them almost a month to spend some time together at the ranch. He said Faith should come to the ranch and bring her horse, Wildflower, to the ranch for the month if she would like. He volunteered to bring a truck and horse trailer to San Angelo to pick up Faith and the horse.

Duke learned that Faith's father owned his own business, which was a well known Feed and Seed store in San Angelo, and that was the reason why she had her own horse. Faith had been in various 4H clubs as a teen and had competed in many events as part of the club's activities. She would be leaving her horse with her siblings if she eventually decided to enter the Army Nurse Corps.

Duke apologized for such a late invitation, but he told her that he had "never in his entire life been so interested in a lady, as to invite her to his ranch on such short notice." He felt that they should use the limited time they had to get to know one another before they were off to their respective commitments.

Faith promised to think about it and discuss it with her parents. They enjoyed their time together in the coffee shop and parted this time on much more favorable terms than they had parted in high school almost five years earlier. Duke then told her again, "he had never in his life ever invited anyone to the ranch before and that this was not just some whim." He hoped she would try and come.

He told Faith that he wanted to get to know her better and they probably only had the next thirty days to do that. He asked her to give the idea some real thought and then he asked her to call him if she was interested. He would not pursue her any longer if she did not feel that there was any chemistry between them.

This put the decision squarely on Faith, as he did not want her to think he was some fly by night guy just wanting a fling. He told her that he was serious in wanting to get to know her better and that life rarely gave couples such a month with an opportunity to see if they were somehow meant to be together. He ended saying, " I believe there is something special about you and I would like to have the time to get to know you better. What's the worse that could happen? You would have a great ranch vacation and return home knowing that at least you tried to get to know me?"

He sealed the deal with a brilliant smile and escorted her back through the lobby to the elevator. He then gave her a light kiss on the check and said, “Please call me”. He then said goodbye and headed to the front of the hotel. She watched him walk away as the elevator doors closed. She liked what she saw.

Chapter Seven: Day Three Alone

The climb to Survival and Notification Day in the USA

April 1970

Duke had made Corporal Turner as comfortable as possible by giving him a morphine shot from the first aid kits he had retrieved once he returned to the young Corporal. He had given the young man a second shot late last night to allow him to get some sleep. The night had seemed long and cold here on this ledge. As soon as Duke awoke, he told Tim that he would eventually try and go for help. But first, they had to both get off this ledge and into the jungle to hide. The Corporal just smiled at the LT and nodded his head slightly. It was clear that he was still in a lot of pain.

Duke had to get them both off the side of this hill if they wanted to survive the next few days, as Duke was sure that the North Vietnamese Army would most assuredly eventually come to this LZ to see their handiwork. He and Tim would have to move quickly to avoid possible capture or death. Duke felt that the only possible reason the enemy had not yet returned, was because they were afraid of a possible stay behind ambush team from the Americans.

The enemy had completed a wonderfully successful attack on the Americans and they probably did not want to spoil that success by walking back into an ambush. But eventually Duke thought that the NVA would come back to the LZ on Hill 786, if for no other reason than to gloat.

Therefore, Duke then got to work setting Tim's broken leg, so that they could both leave this ledge. This was going to be tough. He told Tim that he had to try and set his leg or it would not heal correctly. Tim then acknowledged the LT's remarks and said a very weak "OK". Duke gave the Corporal another morphine shot and then began to re-align the leg into its normal position and then pulled hard to set the bones in alignment. Tim had passed out almost immediately from the pain generated by Duke's pulling and pushing the bones into alignment, which was a blessing to them both as Duke could now pull as hard as necessary.

Duke then cut, tied, and adjusted the branches that he had brought down to the ledge from the Jungle to both sides of Tim's leg to stabilize the leg. Duke had not tried to set the leg the night before, as he wanted to build up some more morphine in Tim's body before attempting such a painful exercise.

He now sat back and surveyed his handiwork on Tim's leg using the branches he had gathered yesterday on the LZ. Thankfully, the bones had not come through the skin and except for a lot of swelling, the leg looked rather normal once Duke got it set and splinted. He had to use Tim's bootlaces and even Tim's belt to help tie the splint onto his leg as the adhesive tape from the first aid kits was just not strong enough to hold the branches tightly against Tim's leg. The branches for Tim's leg were much stronger and non-flexing than the smaller green branches Duke had gathered to repair his own knee.

He knew he had to semi-immobilize his left knee to allow the knee to heal. He did not know if the kneecap was broken or the knee itself was the culprit, but it was clear that the knee could not flex easily and still hold his weight. Once he had set Tim's leg, he then turned his attention to his own knee.

He had chosen green saplings from the jungle for his knee that he knew would flex slightly while still holding the knee in line with his leg. Ranger training really kicked in and he knew just what he had to do. This flexible splint, he hoped, would allow him to walk while flexing the knee only slightly.

He had used the rolls of adhesive tape from the first aid kits to attach the green saplings to each side of his bare knee as he sat beside Tim on the ledge wrapping the adhesive tape completely around his leg above and below the damaged knee. This allowed him more freedom to walk and to slide back and forth on the ledge. Tim's brace had been applied over Tim's fatigue pants to give extra padding to the immobilized leg. Duke applied his own brace under his fatigue trousers so that the adhesive tape would stick to his skin.

Duke sat back and admired all of his handiwork. It looked good and secure. He put his pants back on, and then he waited until Tim woke up. He planned to return to the LZ to begin pulling Tim up and off this ledge. They had to get off this ledge today and hide in the jungle if they wanted to survive this ordeal. But he wanted to do it in the late afternoon when discovery by the enemy might be less of a fear.

Duke had surmised that the enemy had not come to the LZ yet because they were afraid of walking into an American ambush. He thought that might last three or four days, but eventually, the enemy would come to the LZ, he just knew it! They had to be off this ledge by tonight or they could be discovered and then captured or killed. He would have to pull Tim up to the LZ today no matter how much pain the young Corporal had to sustain. Duke found himself repeating his thoughts, as his mind was somewhat befuddled.

Tim came awake about thirty minutes later and asked Duke for some more water. Duke gave him several sips and then told him that Duke had to return to the LZ and then pull on the rope to pull Tim back up and onto the LZ. He would need TIM to help as much as he could. He emphasized to Tim that they had to get into a new hiding place away from this hilltop and the LZ or they might be found and killed by the enemy.

Duke then tied the rope under Tim's arms and then around his chest where Tim could hold onto the rope while using his hands and one good leg to help climb up the hill. He instructed Tim that he was going to pull on the rope and that Tim had to help. That between Duke pulling and Tim attempting to climb, they would be able to get Tim up onto the LZ. Duke then gathered the rucksack, the end of the rope, and all their other gear currently lying on the ledge and then he began to climb back up the hill for what he hoped would be the last time.

Duke finally made it to the top of the hill after another grueling hour of climbing, clawing mostly with his hands as his left knee was not functioning well at all and had started hurting badly and he was currently dragging his left leg up the hill. He was also dragging the long rope tied around his waist and a full rucksack on his back. It was one of the toughest maneuvers he had ever attempted and took all of his stamina.

When he finally got to the top of the hill, he lifted his head slightly above the ground and scanned the LZ again looking for any signs of possible danger. He saw none. The LZ was almost entirely black with charred debris almost everywhere he could see. He again thought that his company must have come back and taken all of the bodies from the LZ right after the explosions while he and Corporal Turner were evidently both unconscious.

He slowly got up and tried to stand but found it was extremely painful because of his left knee. The two climbs up the hill had just about stressed his knee to its breaking point. The splint helped but the knee still hurt badly. It was absolutely on fire with pain. He sat on the empty LZ and ran his hands over the painful knee trying to determine just what was broken, if anything.

He had originally thought that perhaps it was just a pulled ligament, but when he attempted to stand now, it became clear that something was broken or fractured, as the pain was almost unbearable. But the splint did help.

It was now clear that he would not be walking out of here anytime soon. He could barely walk at all and Tim could certainly not walk on his severely broken leg. Duke then untied the Rescue Rope from around his waist and then tied the rope around a tree stump on the side of the LZ. He would then give two strong tugs on the rope to signal Tim that he was about to begin pulling him up. Duke had found a solid tree stump very close to the edge of the LZ. Evidently, the GI's had recently cut down the tree that had once stood there in order to make the LZ safer for the incoming helicopters. He planned to use this tree stump as a type of circular pulley system to help him pull Tim up the hill.

He finished tying the loose end of the rope tightly around the stump so that if Duke had to let go of the rope while Tim was climbing, Tim would still be safe on the other end from falling all the way off the mountain. He then gave Tim the two-tug signal and started pulling on the rope while bracing his good leg and foot against the tree stump.

He talked to Tim the entire time but tried to keep his voice low so it would not travel far in the jungle and alert any enemy where they was located. Tim told Duke that he was ready and Duke then began to pull the rope and Tim tried his best to help climb the hill with his free hands and his one good leg. It was slow going.

Thankfully, Corporal Turner was slightly smaller than the average soldier and probably only weighed about 150 pounds. Tim was now fully awake again and with his leg now set, some of the leg pain had subsided and he could actually help Duke pull him up by using his hands and the other good leg and foot to crawl. It took Duke most of the afternoon to struggle with the rope stopping many times as Tim tried to help crawl his way up the hill.

Eventually, they were both on the LZ and they immediately began moving further into the jungle to find a hiding place where they could wait for any possible rescue. Duke and Tim were both almost completely spent and tired. Duke's body was badly damaged and his ability to work for very long was limited. He would still have to find a stream and fill several canteens with water. He had found four canteens, but only three were intact and would hold water. They would have to share the canteens and refill them often. It was already slightly raining which would also supply them with drinking water if they could find creative ways to collect it.

He returned quickly to the LZ and walked all around the LZ scrounging for anything else that might prove useful to them. He had to work fast as the enemy could already be heading towards their location. He retrieved several more rucksacks including Tim's from the side of the LZ on the other side of the LZ from where they had been blown off the hilltop.

It had been easy to identify Tim's rucksack as it still had the destroyed PRC 25 radio inside the actual rucksack. He sat there simply amazed that Tim's rucksack had landed on the other side of the LZ when the two of them had been lying side by side by the helicopter?

What kind of terrible explosions could have sent them in one direction, and Tim's radio and rucksack in the opposite direction? And Duke's rucksack was not anywhere to be seen on or near the LZ. It must have been blown over the hill and ledge where he had landed. It was just mind-blowing! He now pulled the Radio out of the rucksack and tried to turn it on again to see if it might now be functioning. But when he pulled it out, there was a two-inch diameter hole completely through the radio.

Shrapnel had turned the radio into a plain hunk of useless metal. He threw the radio off to the side and began looking through all of the remaining rucksacks. It was a miracle that Tim was still alive after seeing the hole in the radio, which had been on Tim's back at the time of the explosions.

In the other rucksacks, he found two more small first aid kits that each squad of men always carried, and several more cans of C-rations. He also found two more knives and two more grenades. He quickly dragged everything he could use to their new hiding position in the thick jungle about 100 yards off the LZ

Just a few hours ago on the other side of the world and unbeknownst to First Lieutenant Duke Gabriel, Army Sedans had pulled up to his parent's home on the ranch south of Odessa, Texas, and to all of the other homes of soldiers that had been killed, or missing at the LZ in Vietnam. Officers and Non-Commissioned Officers (NCO's) had given the grim news to all of the parents that their sons had been listed as missing in action, and presumed dead from explosions during combat actions in the Republic of Vietnam.

Duke's parents were completely heartbroken. Duke's father spent the entire night that night in the barn, as he could not comfort his wife from the huge loss. She had to finally be given a sedative to sleep and he could not stand to see her in such a state.

Billy Gabriel, Duke's younger brother, tried to console his father, but the loss was just too great for the rancher and he needed a place to cry without showing his face to other relatives now huddled in the living room of their home.

The 1/327th Battalion Executive Officer, Major Fred Garvey, notified Army Nurse First Lieutenant Faith Gabriel at her unit of assignment, the 85th Evac Hospital in Phu Bai. Faith was devastated. After spending several hours with the chaplain at the hospital, Faith finally sat down to pen a letter to both sets of parents telling them what she thought that they already knew, but assuring them that she would continue to try and find out more details as they became available.

She explained in some detail what 'Missing in action, presumed dead', meant in the military terminology, and tried to give them all hope that Duke might yet be discovered alive.

Meanwhile, Duke was continuing to scrounge anything of value off the top of the hill that might help he and Corporal Turner to survive this ordeal until a rescue party was sent for them. He was already beginning to worry that he had been on the LZ too many times and for far too long a time and might be discovered by the enemy if they were watching this LZ from a distance.

He hurriedly went to every rucksack still in the brush just off the LZ and gathered everything and anything he thought he might need to survive until they were possibly rescued. He just knew that eventually, the army would determine that he and Tim's bodies were not among those they had retrieved and that they would return to look for them.

But they had to survive until that happened. They needed food, water, and shelter and signaling devices should a friendly helicopter come this way. He retrieved and filled four rucksacks with as many items as he could collect and dragged all four of them off the LZ and into the heavy jungle. He then immediately began the task to hide the rucksacks in three different caches almost 50 meters apart and well off the LZ, so that if the enemy discovered one cache, he and Tim might still have others available for their use. He was now sweating profusely and was dead tired, but he kept on working. Thank God Ranger School had taught him well just what he had to do now to survive.

Duke got Tim settled in some thick jungle vegetation well off and away from the LZ. He then went back again to the LZ to take one final look around before returning to Tim's location. Duke had found another small hiding spot further off the side of the main trail, which traveled north and south on the ridgeline and went into action to make the hidden outcropping comfortable for them to hide until he heard any possible rescue birds. He wanted to be close enough to hear any rescue attempt, yet far enough to not be easily discovered by the enemy.

They each ate another cold ration and then Darkness fell over the jungle and Duke rolled up into a ball and slept heavily. He hoped that no wild animals would sense that they were injured and decide to attack. He also worried about any snakes or insects that might attack them after dark. But he had no choice, he badly needed sleep to let his body slowly repair itself and to keep his mind alert the next day.

It would be Duke's longest night yet here in the jungle alone with Tim. They had both been through a lot since the enemy attack and both men were totally spent of energy and any real ability to protect themselves. They were so tired, weak, and dejected. Duke knew that he had to plan for their survival until help came, if it ever did.

If a rescue never came, then they would have to gain strength, let their bodies repair themselves and then start to walk out of this jungle towards friendly forces on Firebase Veghel some 25 walking miles from their current location. Just the thought of such a trek was all but impossible right now. Duke said another small prayer and thanked God that they were both still alive. They both fell into a deep sleep.

Chapter Eight: Summer of 1968
(Two Years Earlier)

Duke returned to the Double Star Ranch the next day after the graduation weekend spent in Austin with his family and began planning for his Army Reporting Date to Fort Benning, Georgia, of 15 July 1968. He was studying the list that had been sent to him with his US Army orders on just what he should bring to the school. He would need one dress uniform and two sets of short sleeve khaki Class B uniforms.

He also needed to see his personal physician and get two injections, a tetanus shot, and a recent booster vaccination, before reporting to the army school. Work uniforms (fatigues), boots, and field clothing would be issued to him at the school. He should also bring one pair of class 'A' (dress) black shoes. He already had all of the uniform items from ROTC and felt he was pretty well prepared.

He reviewed the list several more times to ensure he did not miss anything. But all the while he was thinking about Faith Anderson and whether she might call him at all. He then wondered if he should call her and ask her again, but he had told her to call if she was interested and he did not want to appear to be some kind of stalker. He had to trust that she would call.

Meanwhile, in the suburban mining area of Altoona, Pennsylvania, an event was about to happen that would affect both Duke Gabriel and a thin young man of just 17 years old who had finished his last day of school at the Highland Jones High School in Altoona. The event, while totally separate from Duke Gabriel's present life, would set the stage for someone new to eventually connect into Duke's life just as Faith Anderson had done some years earlier. Events happen everyday that many of us have absolutely no knowledge of, yet these events set forces in motion that will eventually cross paths with our own destiny.

The young teenager in Altoona, Pennsylvania, was on his way home to a home that was not pleasant to live in. He was wondering what he would do for the summer, as he could not stand the idea of being around the house while his father ranted and raved about the bad mining conditions around Altoona, and the lack of work for coal miners.

Timothy Eric Turner hated his home environment and could hardly wait until he was old enough to leave home and join the United States Army. He would not be eighteen until August, which meant he had the summer to wait. His father was a truly depressing man and alcoholic who blamed his failures on everything and everybody except himself. He was unhappy, therefore everyone in the home had to be unhappy. Tim did not know how his mother put up with it all. He really thought that his parents would eventually get a divorce, but each year brought on another challenge and still they stayed together.

Tim wanted to complete his high school education, but only because he wanted to have the High School Diploma before he joined the army. He wanted to change his life forever. He had to get out of the family home before he and his father came to blows. He had already convinced his mother to sign the permission form that would allow him the option to join the army before the age of 18, but even with the permission slip he wanted his high school diploma before he left Altoona, as he might never receive it otherwise. He really wanted to have his diploma in hand before joining the army.

Tim was one of the only older teenagers that still rode the high school bus everyday. They had no money for any car, and Tim had always been an introverted young man who had few friends, as he had no money to attend movies or activities with the other high school kids. He said goodbye to Willie Harold, the school bus driver, who already knew that Tim planned to join the Army.

Tim then climbed the hill toward their small home. He climbed the three stairs to the porch and once again noticed that the screen door was hanging lopsided off its hinges. His dad had promised his mother that he would fix that door today, but as usual, promises from his father meant little when he was drinking. Tim tried to open the front door but it appeared to be jammed. He pushed harder and finally the door gave way and it was then that he saw his mother lying on the floor blocking the movement of the door.

His mother lay in a pool of her own blood at the bottom of the stairs leading to the second floor and her body had blocked the front door from opening correctly. Tim immediately dropped his books inside the front door and went down on his knees next to his mother. A terrible bruise was on her face and she was obviously already dead. She was cold to his touch and had apparently fallen down the front stairs onto the floor just in front of the front door.

He screamed out for his father at the top of his lungs and got no answer. His father was not in the house. Tim ran next door to the neighbors and got Mr. and Mrs. Andrews to come over to the house. The next several hours were spent with Tim sitting in the living room, his books still on the front floor as the police came and went and asked a thousand questions of his father, who had finally returned to the house.

After what seemed like hours, but was probably only minutes, the coroner took his mother's body away. His father told the police that his mother, Betty, often drank too much and probably fell down the stairs. He said he had warned her often not to drink vodka and try to climb the stairs. Tim knew it was all a lie, but the police did not ask him anything as he sat quietly crying in the living room.

After everyone had left the home, his father told Tim that Tim had better find a job this summer, as Joe would need help keeping the house rent paid now that Tim's mother would not be working as a maid anymore. His father expressed little remorse or sympathy for his mother, and just told Tim that he knew it would happen eventually.

Timothy hated his father, and he suspected that his mother had not fallen down the stairs but was pushed down the stairs. Such were the usual actions of his father hitting his mother daily. That very night, Tim quietly packed a suitcase, gathered the forms for the army that his mother had already signed, and after his father fell asleep, Tim left the home never to return.

He walked all night to downtown Altoona and was sitting beside the army enlistment office door when they opened early the next morning. He signed all the papers, took the physical and was on a bus toward Harrisburg, Pennsylvania by midday. He had never looked back and was eventually trained as an infantryman and would be sent to Vietnam in 1969.

Over the next year at Fort Benning, Georgia, Tim Turner managed to get his high school diploma sent to him by requesting it through the US Army Education Center at Fort Benning. He was a bright young man and had no trouble completing the army requirements for several military occupational categories

By the next summer of 1969, Tim was assigned to the First Platoon, D Company, 1/327th Battalion, 101st Airborne Division in the Republic of Vietnam as a Specialist Fourth Class in the Army Infantry. He had finally turned eighteen and he was now a full-fledged infantryman. His Platoon Leader would soon be First Lieutenant Adam Duke Gabriel, a leader that would change and influence the rest of Tim's life as no one had ever done before.

The Gabriel family had arrived back at the Double Star Ranch after the graduation ceremony late the next Monday afternoon in June 1968. Everyone had immediately gone back to the daily routines and Duke was organizing various articles for his trip to Fort Benning. Monday night's supper was a normal ranch supper held in the large dining room at the ranch with a buffet set up for all of the ranch hands and cowboys. Ranch life was an ever-constant cycle of work, meals, and more work. Ranching was an absolute full-time job of taking care of cattle, horses, assorted pets, and over 40 cowboys at any given time. The work never stopped.

Duke spent Tuesday riding several ranges and helping to move stock from one pasture to another. He had to admit that he loved the ranch and its constant motion. He was going to miss this place when he went off to the Army at Fort Benning, next month, but Faith Anderson was never far from his mind. He had hoped that Faith would call him as soon as he returned to the ranch, but she had not. He had just about decided that Faith was not going to call him and that he should get his act together and move forward with his life.

Perhaps Duke could revisit his prospects with Faith Anderson once he completed his army training. After all, he had just approached her this past weekend, and she was probably busy with her own schedule. He did find her incredibly attractive and he had to wonder what planet he had been on when he had let her get away back in high school? What was he thinking back then? But, he knew that football and the ranch were his only interests back then.

Duke rode back to the main barn and unsaddled his horse, Rustler. It had felt really good to be in the saddle today. He had forgotten just how much he loved riding Rustler, his horse of many years. He brushed down the horse and stored the bridle and his handmade saddle in the tack room. The saddle, like his boots, had his name 'DUKE" leather tooled into the rear of the seat. He loved the hand-tooled Mexican saddle, which had been a Christmas Present from his parents in 1964 after his 18th Birthday and in celebration of his senior year in high school.

He then walked up to the main house looking forward to a hot shower and perhaps a cold beer before supper. He climbed the back stairs to the boot room that his mother had insisted be installed before the men of the family walked through the home leaving horse and cattle dung all over her carpets. He used the boot cleaning brushes that were permanently installed on the back stairs. They had been designed and installed in such a manner that all you had to do was place your boot into the brush holder and pull the boot back through the form and the brushes would do their work of removing debris from the sole and sides of the boot.

It was not a perfect device, but it did take the majority of debris off the bottom and sides of the boot. The men of the house would then enter the boot room and take off their work boots and then put on their comfort boots that were stored in the room on various shelves. This kept the house cleaner, the women happier, and the men out of trouble. This routine never changed for the men of the Gabriel family entering their mother's home.

The cowboys and ranch hands likewise had a similar boot cleaning devise mounted on the stairs to the large ranch dining room attached to the other side of the house. But the difference was, that once the boots were brushed, the Cowboys just entered the dining room whose floors were made of barn lumber and were hosed down every evening after the three meals each day. No cowboy from the ranch ever actually entered the main ranch house unless specifically invited by the family.

Duke entered the kitchen and gave his mom a hug, as she was busy organizing the upcoming dinner as she did almost every night at the ranch. They had a fulltime cook staff employed and Mrs. Gabriel was not actually needed in the kitchen on a daily basis, but Dorothy Gabriel still enjoyed her role as 'Queen' of the Double Star Ranch.

Dorothy accepted Duke's hug and asked him how his day had gone? Duke responded, "Great Mom, Rustler was very glad to be riding the fences again." Dorothy then said, "Well, what about Duke Gabriel, did he also enjoy riding the fences?" Duke laughed and said, "Yep, I must admit I love the ranch and riding the various pastures."

Dorothy let he son loose and then said, "There is a note by the phone for you." Duke raised an eyebrow and said, "From anyone I know?" Dorothy said while smiling, "I believe it's from that young lady you invited here when we were all at the graduation?" Duke smiled and immediately walked to the hallway table and picked up the note.

The housekeeper had left the note on the table next to the phone, and it said, " Please return a call to Miss. Faith Anderson at the number she gave you on graduation day." Duke immediately took out his wallet and pulled Faith's number from his wallet and began to dial the telephone.

Mrs. Alice Anderson answered the phone and Duke then asked to speak with Faith. Faith came on the line and Duke said, "This is Duke Gabriel, and I'm sorry I'm so late in calling but I have been out on the range all day." Faith giggled slightly and said, "Well I guess that song 'Home on the Range' applies to every cowboy in Texas?" Duke smiled to himself and said, "Yep, that's me, a regular John Wayne." Faith said, "Well, I'll take your word for it, but I was really wondering if your invitation to come to the ranch for a couple of days was still in effect?"

Duke sat down next to the table where the phone was located, and said, "By all means, when would you like to visit?" Faith said, "Well I have about ten days available and I would love to come and bring my horse, Wildflower, if that's possible? I can bring the horse in his horse trailer if I drive my Dad's pickup truck."

Duke immediately said, "That's great, but I will be glad to come and pick you both up with my truck, but we can use your trailer if Wildflower is more comfortable in your trailer?" Faith said, "That would be nice, and Wildflower takes to any trailer just fine. Duke then said, "I could come tomorrow if that was alright with you and your folks?"

Faith told Duke that she would need a day to get organized but that he could pick them up on Thursday if that was OK with Duke? Duke then said, "It's a Date, or I should say, I will be there Thursday at noon if that is OK?" Faith then said that would be fine and then she said, "My sixteen-year-old brother Alex wants to come along if that would be ok?" Duke said, "Sure, does he also have his own horse?"

Faith then explained that her younger brother, Alex, did not yet have a horse. Her father had planned for Alex to take care of Faith's horse, Wildflower, once Faith left for her tentatively planned Army Medical Officer Training at the end of the summer. Duke told her that her brother, Alex, was most welcome and that he could provide a nice horse for Alex once he got to the ranch.

Faith also asked if they could use the guest cabin that Duke had described and he said "yes." They talked for a few more minutes together and then Duke hung up and then let loose a "cheer" that was loud enough that his mother came around the corner to see what was going on. He sheepishly looked at his mom and said, "Faith and her brother, Alex, are coming to the Ranch on Thursday for a visit." Dorothy smiled at her son and said, "This girl must be someone really special?" Duke just smiled and said, "Well, she the best thing that's happened to me in a long time!"

He then told his mother all about his invitation and Faith's acceptance. His mother said, "Well, you had better get over to that cabin and clean the place up if you are going to expect a young lady to take up residence there? The last time I looked, it was pretty dirty." Duke said, "No problem mom, I'm on it". That night after supper, Duke actually cleaned the little cabin for the first time in his life. It was very clear to his mother that this young lady, Faith, must be really important to Duke.

The cabin needed a bit more cleaning than Duke had expected and he was glad he had the entire day Wednesday to clean it up. He even mopped all of the wood floors and his mother brought fresh linen to the cabin to change the beds and fresh towels for the bathrooms. The cabin was quite nice and had been used by the family as guest quarters for years.

It had two complete bedrooms, each with its own bath, and a large central room with a huge stone fireplace. It also had a small galley kitchen that contained a sink, dishwasher, refrigerator, small stove, and even a new Amana state of the art microwave oven, which had just become available in 1967. The kitchen was never really designed to cook large meals, but it was none-the-less very usable and comfortable and also had a new Silex brand coffee pot and toaster.

The cabin had been designed to allow those staying at the ranch as guests to make their own breakfast if they so desired, but it was expected that guests would come to the main ranch house for suppers. Duke spent the entire day, Wednesday, getting the cabin ready for Faith and her brother. He even went to the local store and bought some groceries and went about stocking the kitchen.

He spent the entire day making the cabin warm and inviting even down to putting some flowers in a vase on the kitchen table, and adding milk, butter, and soft drinks in the refrigerator. He had also bought English Muffins, bread, and two types of cereal for the kitchen. His mother came over to help and was amazed at what her son had done. She knew immediately that this young lady must be very special to Duke, as he had never before done such a thing.

Duke then washed the newest ranch truck and attached his father's best horse trailer onto the hitch. It was a truly impressive truck and trailer combination with the ranch logos on the doors and on the sides of the dual horse trailer. They used the expensive rig to take prized livestock to various completions throughout the state. His father helped him hitch the trailer and check out the rig before Duke left the ranch. His father asked him at least two times to explain his infatuation with the young lady, but never got a truly straight answer. Roger Gabriel eventually went back to the main house and told his wife, Dorothy that "their son was in love."

Early Thursday morning Duke was off to the town of San Angelo, about 50 miles east of Odessa to pick up Faith, Wildflower, and her brother Alex. He had no problem finding the Anderson home in the outskirts of San Angelo and parked the truck and trailer next to the small barn on the property. It was clear to him now that his new romantic interest was, in fact, a country gal, complete from a home with a small barn. Things were definitely looking up.

He climbed down from the large truck and began walking toward the house. A sweet voice made him turnaround, as Faith came out of the barn leading Wildflower, an Indian painted pony, by a halter. Duke turned around and headed towards the duo. Faith was smiling and said, "Well, Hello there, Cowboy!" Duke put a finger to his hat and lowered his head as he said, "Well, howdy there ma'am, it certainly is a wonderful day!"

Faith laughed and said, "You handle that cowboy talk well." He laughed and came up beside her and took Wildflower's halter in hand. Faith was about to warn him that Wildflower was named "Wild" for a reason, but the horse immediately proved her wrong, as the small painted filly nuzzled right into Duke's hand. Faith said, "Well, that is absolutely amazing! I have never seen Wildflower make a friend so fast."

Duke just smiled and said, "Well, I have a nice way with the ladies." Faith laughed again as she said,

"Well you certainly have the lingo and the swagger down pat!" Duke just smiled and stroked the horse as he looked at Faith and said, "Why, you are a real pretty little filly." Faith silently wondered if he was talking to the horse or to her, and it was clear he was not going to say which? They walked toward the horse trailer attached to the truck as Faith said, "I thought you were going to take our trailer?" Duke then said, "Well, this truck works best with the custom trailer, so I brought both, I hope that is OK?"

Faith assured him that it was fine just as her brother Alex came bounding out of the house and ran up to the truck. Alex held out his hand and said, "I'm Alex Anderson and I am very glad to meet you, Mr. Gabriel." Duke said, "Well, glad to meet you too Alex, and I am just 'Duke' to my friends." Alex beamed at being accepted by the rough looking cowboy and immediately asked if he could be of help? Duke told the young man "Sure, why don't you lead Wildflower here up into the trailer if she will listen to you" Alex said, "Sure thing, Duke, and took hold of the halter of the horse."

Faith then asked Duke to come up to the house and meet her mom before they loaded their bags. Duke followed her up onto the porch and immediately looked around for the boot brush but found none on the steps. He said, "My mom does not allow us into the house without first cleaning off our boots." Faith said, "We are a bit more relaxed here and there is a heavy rug inside the door for wiping your boots."

Duke took off his hat as he walked through the front door, wiped his boots on the rough door carpet, and followed Faith into the kitchen to meet her mom. He soon learned that her father was currently at the feed store in town, and that he and his wife shared the duties at the store.

Faith's Mom, Alice, liked Duke almost immediately because of his strong country manners and gestures. She indicated that they should both take a seat at the kitchen table and she asked Duke if he would like some coffee and a cinnamon bun? Duke said, "Why sure Ma'am, that would be great!" The next 15 minutes were spent drinking their coffee and talking while Duke enjoyed and scarfed down, not one, but three of her wonderful cinnamon rolls.

Alex came inside the kitchen and announced that he had loaded the horse and the gear along with his and his sister's bags. Everyone talked for a few more minutes and then Faith told her mom they needed to get going, and Alice told everyone to have a safe trip and escorted them out onto the porch. Faith's mom quietly whispered into Faith's ear that "I know you are now of age, but please be careful and don't give away the farm before the man has bought a ring for your finger." Faith smiled at her mother and said, "Mom, its just a holiday at a ranch, nothing more yet."

The new ranch pickup truck Duke had brought to Anderson's farm had only one front bench seat, so Duke gave Faith a hand up into the cab and then Alex took the shotgun position next to the passenger side window. This placed Faith extremely close to Duke as he drove the vehicle. Duke loved it! He was glad that Alex was coming along on the trip. The three young people drove the 50 some miles back to the Double Star Ranch talking the entire way about a myriad of topics. Alex was just thrilled to be on his way to a real cattle ranch!

Once back at the Double Star, Wildflower was given her own stall in the main barn, and Faith had a moment with Wildflower alone as the men gathered Wildflower's saddle and equipment. Faith stroked the side of Wildflower's pole and whispered quietly to the horse, "Well, you have never let anyone else just take your bridle and walk you out to a horse trailer. I can only assume that you evidently like Duke Gabriel don't you?" The horse seemed to nod its head gently as Faith stroked and talked to the horse. Faith then said, "Well I kind of like him too!"

Duke then took the Anderson siblings to the ranch guest cabin to get settled. Both siblings were ecstatic with the accommodations, which were much better than they had ever expected. Alex had expected to find a plain bunkhouse with hard bunks, not a fancy guest cabin that looked better than a hotel suite! Faith and Alex were left in the cabin and changed clothes for supper and then joined the extended family in the main house for supper.

Dorothy Gabriel had done nothing extra for the evening meal and the menu that evening was much the same almost every night. Every meal almost always was the same assortment of meat, potatoes, vegetables, salad, and dessert. The only exception was an occasional Italian night, which gave all the cowboys spaghetti, meatballs, lasagna, and Italian salad. Ranch hands needed solid food and plenty of it, as the work on the ranch was hard and physically demanding every day. The caloric count was always sky high on Dorothy's table.

Faith and Alex Anderson had never seen such large food portions as was displayed that evening on the side buffet tables. The Gabriel family ate most nights with the ranch hands in the main dining room, the only difference being that the family had a separate roundtable in one corner of the room while all the ranch hands ate at long picnic style tables extended throughout the extremely large room.

After supper, Duke took Alex to the main barn and introduced him to Dwayne Hobbs, the ranch foreman. Dwayne, called simply 'Hobbs' by almost everyone, immediately took young Alex under his wing for the rest of his stay at the ranch. Hobbs would get the boy a horse, saddle, equipment, and training on how to be a real ranch hand. Alex was in heaven. He would spend the next week riding the ranges and learning everything about the ranch. Duke was also overjoyed, as this left him time alone with Faith to get to know her better without having to drag her little brother around all day like a puppy. It was what he called a win-win proposition!

The next week was one of the best weeks in Adam Duke Gabriel's life. There was no doubt that he was falling hard for the young lady by his side that week. They talked about everything as Faith rode with Duke almost everywhere on the ranch that week as Duke did his normal ranch work. They soon fell into a regular routine that included breakfast together, then Duke would saddle the horses for the day's work, while Faith would pack a basket for their lunch and fill three thermos bottles with coffee and Iced Tea.

Duke and Faith would then ride out onto the ranch and be together the entire day while Duke checked fences, cattle herds, and pastures. Meanwhile Alex awoke everyday at daylight and headed for the barn to meet Hobbs. He would then join the ranch cowboys on whatever job they had that day. He loved it!

The next Saturday night, all of the ranch hands and members of the Gabriel family went to a neighboring ranch for a 'Hay Bale' Dance that was held every summer rotating between ranches in the area. Duke led Faith out onto to the temporary dance floor and they had a wonderful night together doing the line dances and square dances that were featured that evening. Alex had discovered a neighbor girl Kathy that caught his eye, and was busy trying to keep from falling over his own feet as she taught him country line dancing.

When the week came to an end, Duke asked Faith and Alex to stay for another week, and both agreed. They called their folks and told them that they wanted to stay another week and both were pleased when it could all be worked out.

The second week would establish a relationship between Faith and Duke that would never again be severed. The second Tuesday of the Anderson siblings visit brought the annual roundup on the Double Star Ranch. Alex asked his sister if he could go on the roundup over the next two nights with the ranch cowboys out on the range, and she acquiesced.

That gave the lovebirds two nights of privacy they had not had the first week of the Anderson visit. Duke spent the two nights in the cabin with Faith and nature had managed to take its course. They were both over twenty one and they were falling in love. Faith suspected that this might happen and had planned birth control accordingly.

Their first lovemaking was absolutely surreal in its intensity and both immediately knew that they had found their special someone forever. That night, Duke sat on the couch in the guest cabin while Faith lay with her head in his lap as they talked late into the night. The sensual feelings of such a simple act of love for another human being were amazing to them both. Adam Duke Gabriel just knew that he had found his soul mate.

By the end of the second week, Faith and Duke had completely fallen in love with one another and were already talking about a possible engagement party come Christmas time, which would be their next possible break from their army training courses and probably their first opportunity to be together again.

Faith and Alex said their goodbyes to the Gabriel family and Alex gave a strong handshake to both Hobbs and Duke at being invited to the ranch. Alex had grown into a natural cowboy during his two weeks at the ranch and Hobbs had told him that he could have a summer job there next summer if he wanted to come. Alex was thrilled.

Faith had tears in her eyes as she hugged Adam and also when saying goodbye to Dorothy and Rodger Gabriel. Duke and Alex loaded Wildflower back into the horse trailer and Alex loaded the travel bags into the pickup truck for the trip back home. Duke stopped midway back to the Anderson Farm at a very nice restaurant along the way and the three had a wonderful early supper together before Duke dropped them off at their farm that evening.

Chapter Nine: Day Four Alone

Hill 786, Republic of Vietnam

Duke was shivering and cold. The weather in Vietnam was never really cold, but it seemed colder when it rained, as the temperature could drop as far as fifty-five degrees Fahrenheit. It was such a morning on Hill 786 just 100 yards off the LZ, where they were currently hiding.

Normally, he would just roll his sleeves down on his jungle fatigues and move around until he warmed up, but huddled in his little outcropping nest just off the major ridgeline, kept him from moving quickly to warm up. Once again he had to concentrate on just where he was and why he and Tim were alone together. The past three days of personal memories quickly returned and flooded his mind. He immediately came to full alert and began listening to the jungle's sounds around him to ensure that they were still alone.

Duke had found two poncho liners (Light nylon camouflaged blankets) in the Army rucksacks he had recently moved and used them to wrap Tim, as Tim was not doing well. Tim had absolutely exhausted himself in the climb up from the ledge the day before and lay shivering in the leaves. Duke managed to make some hot coffee from some packets of coffee, water, and heat tabs (hard fuel bars) he had found among the LZ rucksacks and was currently feeding the hot liquid to Tim's mouth, which was so badly cut that half of the liquid escaped before he could ingest it. Tim looked up at Duke with tears in his eyes and said, "Thank you so much for not leaving me. I did not want to die alone on that ledge."

It broke Duke up to see the young man so afraid. Duke said, "Tim, you are not going to die alone or any other way. We are going to get out of this alive, both of us!" Tim then said, "I don't know about that, as I feel awful and I'm obviously a drag on your ability to get out of here." Duke told him that they were brothers and that they would both get out of here alive, it just might take some time and Tim had to remain positive and help him by healing. Duke told Tim that he had to trust him.

Duke got Tim well bundled in the two poncho liners for warmth and then took the remainder of the morning to literally crawl down to the bottom of the ridgeline where he found a small stream and was able to bathe himself, rinse the blood off his body and uniform and fill three canteens.

Unfortunately, he could not bring Tim down to this stream, as it would be too dangerous if they were discovered. Tim was utterly unable to move quickly should they need to hide somewhere by the stream if they were discovered there. He would have to wash Tim in their current hiding place and there was no way that he had enough strength to carry Tim down to the stream.

Duke had taken off his clothes to bathe and then discovered that he had severe burns all over his back, chest, and torso. He had evidently just not felt the additional pain of the burns, because of the overriding pain of his knee. But when he entered the water, the burns came alive and the pain was almost unbearable. He then painfully and slowly washed his body and his clothes in the stream. He wanted to wash with the soap that he had found to keep from getting an infection in any of these burns and wounds.

He would once again have to look through the first aid kits and see if there were any antiseptic or ointments he might be able to spread over some of the worst burns that both he and Tim now had all over their bodies.

Duke was absolutely spent of all energy by the time he got back up the hill to their hideaway. He helped Tim to drink some water and then they both fell asleep and did not wake again until after midday. At that very moment, it began to rain again. The rain started coming stronger and Duke decided that it was now time for Tim to wash using the water that the Lord was now providing.

Duke explained to Tim that he had to wash so that his burns would not become infected. The day had warmed up considerably and was now much more comfortable for Tim as he was no longer shivering. Duke had retrieved the bar of soap from a rucksack on the LZ and proceeded to help Tim out of his clothes and onto some soft leaves and branches that Duke had managed to lay out for the sponge bath. Duke had to remove the leg brace for a few minutes so that Tim could slide off his trousers. As the rain fell, Tim and Duke began soaping up Tim's body.

Duke then told Tim to use the soap to wash his genitals and waist area very well, as Duke was afraid of Tim developing the severe fungal rash that was so common to soldiers in Vietnam. He had to remain as clean as possible. Tim managed to wash in his private areas and then Duke told him that he would apply a heavy layer of powder later after the rain stopped. He had found powder to be the best protection to help prevent sweating in the body's tightest areas.

After Tim was bathed as best that they both could do, Duke helped the young Corporal back into his jungle fatigues that Duke had already washed off to the side in a steel helmet liner the best he could, while Tim was bathing himself. Duke then reapplied the splints to each side of Tim's wet pant legs and the young soldier leaned back against a tree and smiled saying, "I feel much better already."

The rain finally stopped an hour later and the skies began to clear once again as often happened here in the jungles of Vietnam. One minute it was storming and cool and the next minute it was hot as Hell. The sun came out and they were both completely dry within minutes as their jungle fatigues had been designed to dry very quickly.

Duke then took out his P38 C-ration can opener that was on a chain around his neck along with his dog tags and opened two C-ration cans of beef and potatoes and he and Tim scarfed drown their first real meal in their new hiding place. They ate the meal in almost record time.

They were both very hungry and Duke almost reached for another can but then decided they would need to spread out the rations and decided not to eat another can. They had to have food discipline if they were to survive. He began to think about other possible food sources here in the jungle. He would need to supplement the C-rations that they had. He knew that he had seen bananas in the jungle, but neither he nor Tim could remember if any were in this immediate area.

He knew that bananas were plentiful in Vietnam and that they grew year round, and bananas were just about the only food source that grew closer to the ground where they could be harvested easily. Coconuts were also plentiful in the jungle, but there was absolutely no way he or Tim was going to be able to climb to the height required to get any of the fruit. But they could search around the trees to look for fallen coconuts, which might be collected for food.

They could also eat insects and grubs, but the idea of eating those turned his stomach. But he remembered that Ranger School instructors had taught that insects and grubs were a great source of protein if you got over your basic instinct not to eat them. It would depend on just how desperate they might become.

He took stock of their meager supplies and began planning for just how they would survive until rescue came. He just knew that the company would return to look for them once they realized he and Corporal Turner were both missing in action. He then started thinking that he should probably start a calendar so that they could remember the date.

He knew that the mortar attack had happened on the 30th of March 1970, so today had to be the second or third of April. He laughed to himself that he had passed right over April fool's day and that any friends that knew him now probably considered him the 'April Fool' himself? After all, he had allowed his unit to stumble into that LZ Mortar ambush. He blamed himself for the entire action. Duke always took full responsibility for all of his leadership actions, whether he was at a fault or not. He was their leader; therefore, by his definition he was at fault.

He had found a pen among the army rucksack remains on the LZ and used a brown cardboard C-ration box to begin his handwritten calendar. He tried to walk around a little to exercise his knee, but soon sat back down as the knee was very painful and he knew that walking any measurable distance was not going to be easy at all. Especially here in the mountains where every trail was rough and went up or down and rarely was flat in nature. Besides, he absolutely could not carry Tim with his broken knee and he could not leave the young soldier alone.

Duke pulled out his map that was still inside his shirt, and once again noted just where they were located. He knew that his current location was about 15 clicks, (15 Kilometers), from Firebase Veghel, his battalion's headquarters base. That was about nine miles as the crow flies and much further, maybe twice that distance when one added in the ups and downs of elevation moving through this mountainous area of Vietnam.

He also knew he and Tim could not walk over fifteen to twenty miles on foot in the current condition of their bodies. They both hurt everywhere there was a muscle that could yell. But staying where he was could also be dangerous. Duke decided not to take any more morphine pain shots himself. He had to stay alert and Tim was in much more pain than Duke.

The morphine had to be saved for Tim. Sooner or later the enemy would come back to the LZ hilltop to set eyes on the actual damage they had done to the US Army. They should probably move again to ensure they were not discovered, but where would they move? Duke needed to be where they could still watch and signal the LZ in case a rescue party came there.

So he had a real dilemma. Should he stay here and hope for his unit to return to hunt for him, or should he move further away to ensure their safety should the enemy show up here instead? Duke finally decided that they had to do both. He immediately decided that he should fashion several clues to leave on the LZ that would alert any friendly forces that they were still alive but that he would then move them both a bit further away from the LZ, so as to gain protection should the enemy show up here.

He managed to limp back to the LZ, and he then began to 'stage' the LZ in the way that would tell his company brothers that he was still alive. First, he threw a couple empty C-Ration cans onto the side of the LZ. Freshly opened cans would indicate that someone had eaten a C-Ration on the LZ. He also took a stick and wrote the words, "Home on the Range" on the LZ, which he hoped would tell anyone in his company that the Texas Cowboy was still alive and living in the jungle.

He then left the LZ and began to look for a physical position where he and Tim could monitor the LZ without exposing themselves to any enemy that might show up here. That was going to be a problem. Since the LZ was on the top of the hill, they would have to go to another nearby hill in order to keep the LZ in sight, while keeping themselves safe from discovery. This was going to be extremely difficult. His body hurt all over, and the idea of leaving his food caches also gave him pause, but staying beside this well-worn trail was just too dangerous right now.

He then packed some food items in his cargo pockets and rucksack and then assisted Tim to walk holding Tim's weight on his good leg and slowing walked towards the next hilltop. It took almost three hours for them to get to the next hilltop. During their trek, Duke used a branch to drag behind him as he stopped often and walked back and forth on the trail to help eliminate any tracks they had made. He had once seen a cowboy in a movie drag a branch behind his horse to eliminate tracks so he did the next best thing and just dragged the branch behind him. He had to try and erase any signs of their existence.

Moving was extremely slow and cumbersome. It took all the energy they had to just move at all, let alone to climb down one hill and then up to the next hilltop. It took them the remainder of the afternoon to move themselves only a couple of hundred yards. When they finally got to a point where they could still see the old

LZ, yet were far enough away as to not be easily detected, Duke collapsed into a sweaty heap. He was totally exhausted and now he knew for a fact that there was absolutely no way that they could walk out of this jungle anytime soon. Their bodies would have to heal before attempting any great trek out of the jungle.

He had kept his eyes open as he walked to the next hilltop looking for anything that he might be able to eat. He had never really looked to his left and right while walking through the jungle before the explosion as his food was already in his rucksack. But now he had to learn to hunt for food to save their meager rations. He saw several coconut trees with coconuts clearly visible up in the tall branches, but there was absolutely no way they were going to climb any tree in their current condition.

Perhaps he could gather a few in a month or two if he and Tim were still out here that long and if his knee healed itself? Until then he could only look around the trees to find any possible fallen nuts. But, he did see for the first time several banana trees. He had never noticed them before as the bananas were the same green color as the foliage of the tree and were almost invisible unless you were actually looking for them.

He had heard that bananas grew year round in Vietnam but had never really considered looking for them or eating them. But now, they could be a lifesaver! He also remembered someone telling him that snakes and spiders also loved bananas and that he should be careful when trying to pick any wild bananas.

He picked several bananas while carefully looking around for any snakes or spiders, but saw none in this particular area. The bananas were not very ripe and the first one he attempted to eat was pretty sour. He would have to let them ripen in the sun before he attempted to eat another one. The day ended with more frustration over their lack of food and water and with no signs of any US soldiers coming to their rescue anytime soon. Surely by now, they knew they were not among the dead?

Back at Camp Eagle, Faith had become very frustrated at not hearing more from Major Garvey about the loss of the First Platoon soldiers. He had promised to return with more news but had yet to come back to the 85th hospital. She just had to know what had happened and if any other news was going to be forthcoming. She decided she must start asking more questions.

Chapter Ten: The Path to Vietnam
(Two Years Earlier)
Summer 1968

The trip back to the Double Star Ranch was quiet and allowed Duke to reflect on the past two weeks with Faith. He just knew that he was completely smitten with Faith and her truly wonderful personality. He had never been one to particularly chase girls or even think much about dating, but Faith brought out the strong natural instincts of love, protection, and adoration. He needed to solidify their relationship soon before someone else might find out just how utterly fantastic Faith was as a possible life mate.

The next two months were busy for both Duke and Faith. Duke left the ranch for his Army Basic Training Course at Fort Benning on July 12th, 1968. By mid-September he had graduated from the six-week Basic Officer Course and was then sent to Ranger Training at Camp Darby, Fort Benning to begin the nine-week Ranger Course. The Ranger Course would keep him busy until he was scheduled for Army Airborne Training in November. By the time the Christmas Break would come around on or about 15

December, Duke hoped to be a fully qualified Airborne Ranger Lieutenant in the United States Army.

Meanwhile, Faith had taken a job position as an emergency room nurse with the local hospital in San Angelo, Texas. She had rented a small apartment close to the hospital and was enjoying her first real job as a nurse. She was still exploring the possibility of joining the army reserves as a nurse but had not made any real decision as her new job was taking most of her time.

Ranger training was much more difficult than Duke had expected. It challenged him in every way both physically and mentally. He had never before taken on such a challenge. Ranger school made every man acutely aware of his strengths and weaknesses. He was assigned a ranger buddy, Danny Butler, as was everyone else, and the two men grew closer to each other than Duke had ever been to any other man in his entire life.

Survival in ranger school meant survival for both yourself and your ranger buddy. No one could leave a ranger buddy behind. Duke and Danny only had a few hours break between each of the three phases of training and Duke used those hours to write to Faith, his parents, and to eat as much as humanly possible before the next phase of training. He and Danny literally went from one restaurant to the next eating everything they could before the eight hours of freedom ended and they had to report back for the next phase of Ranger School.

Ranger school was divided into three phases of three weeks each, with each phase taught in a different challenging location. Phase one was taught at Camp Darby on Fort Benning. Phase two was taught in the mountains of Northern Georgia and phase three was taught in the swamps of the Florida panhandle. It taught everyone to survive in three extreme environments.

The ranger instructors used food as both the reward and discipline system during training. Stress was added by physically demanding training while food or the lack thereof, became the single thought in most students' minds. By the time Duke had completed ranger school, he had lost almost 20 pounds on his body that was already lean by any imagination.

He started Airborne (Parachute) training the very next week and found it to be easy in comparison to the ranger course. By mid-December, he was dreaming about returning home to the Double Star Ranch and the huge buffets laid out for every meal. In fact, the ranch supper meal buffets consumed most of his recent thoughts.

Faith Anderson was soon promoted to a key position on the hospital nursing staff. Her outstanding nursing abilities had been quickly recognized by superiors, and within just 90 days, she had been made the deputy head of nursing on the emergency room staff. She loved the new job and found nursing both demanding and highly rewarding.

She missed Duke tremendously and wrote many letters to him when she had the opportunity. She had only received four letters from Duke since she and Alex had left the ranch last summer. It was now almost Thanksgiving and she longed to hear from Duke again. She knew that his army training was very demanding, so she did understand the lack of communication, but she longed to see and hold him again.

Duke Gabriel graduated from Army Airborne training on 15 December 1968 and headed immediately to the Columbus, Georgia Airport for a flight home to Texas. He had called Faith from the pay phone next to the training barracks his last night at Fort Benning and had given her his flight numbers, times, and arrival information.

He was to return to Fort Benning after the holidays to be assigned to the student detachment as a training officer until he received his next orders, which were expected to be to Vietnam sometime in the late summer of 1969. But his training phase was finally over, and now he would have more time to see and be with Faith. He intended to use that time to the most advantage to be with Faith, to love Faith, and to propose to Faith as soon as possible. He just knew that she was his entire future.

Faith met Duke at the San Angelo Airport and the two hugged and kissed for several minutes while waiting for Duke's duffle bag and luggage to be delivered. Duke had a thirty-day leave after his training before he had to report for his next assignment at Fort Benning. He spent the first week of that leave at Faith's apartment in San Angelo and had called his parents several times vowing to return home for Christmas. Faith was able to take holiday vacation from the hospital and accompanied Duke back to the Double Star Ranch for Christmas.

On the night before they actually left San Angelo, Duke proposed to Faith at a local restaurant and gave Faith a beautiful solitaire diamond ring. They were officially engaged. Faith's family was ecstatic with the news and hugged them both over the news the next morning. Duke then loaded Faith's Jeep with their bags and the two of them drove to the Double Star Ranch the next day. Rodger and Dorothy Gabriel were shocked when they got the news that the 'Duke' was engaged. Dorothy took the news well, as she just knew her boy had been smitten with Faith Anderson. But Rodger and Hobbs were floored! They thought Duke was a confirmed bachelor.

Duke was the brunt of several jokes over the next few days by many Double Star ranch hands that kept telling him that living with a horse was much easier than living with a woman. He took their jabs well, knowing that they were really quite pleased for him, but they had to maintain the cowboy mystic of strength and loneliness.

He and Faith took many rides on the ranch over the next week as they talked and planned for their future. They saw a future for them both on the ranch, but Duke still had his army obligation and Faith had decided to follow him in those assignments until they could both return to the Double Star Ranch and put down permanent roots.

Duke and Faith made love almost every night of their week together before Christmas. They were definitely committed in this relationship and had even discussed whether they should get married before Duke got orders for Vietnam, which was always a looming monster on the horizon. They finally decided that they should plan a wedding for June 1969 as Faith, in particular, could not stand the idea of not being married to Duke Gabriel before he left for Vietnam. She wanted to be sure that she would be notified should he be wounded or injured and the only way to assure that was to be an official spouse so that she would be on his next of kin forms.

They discussed their future at length and finally announced a tentative wedding date for 6 June 1969. They wanted to get married on the Double Star Ranch and have a western wedding and reception in the barn among all their family members and cowboys at the ranch. Duke would have to try and get the date approved by his superiors in the army and Faith would try and clear her calendar at the San Angelo Hospital for the event. The ranch had enough guest bedrooms for almost all of their relatives and special friends and only a few people would have to be lodged at neighboring ranches, which Rodger and Dorothy Gabriel could arrange.

Christmas was a wonderful experience for everyone at the Double Star Ranch. Rodger and Dorothy Gabriel always tried to make the holidays extra special for the ranch hands and cowboys. This meant erecting a huge Christmas 'Tree' in the open and mowed cantonment area between the barn and the main house and with decorations and lights hung almost everywhere.

Each Ranch Hand and Cowboy on the ranch would get a Christmas bonus check and a Christmas stocking containing thoughtful gifts from Dorothy and Rodger. The Christmas stockings were all hung along the side of the main dining room for all to see a week before Christmas. Dorothy and Faith then filled the stockings with candy, small gifts, a pocket knife, and candy canes on Christmas Eve, so that they would all be full of goodies for Christmas morning. Faith just loved the thoughtfulness of the gestures made by the family.

Christmas was very special for Duke and Faith that year. Their lives together were just starting and they had such dreams for the future. The next six months were going to be very difficult for them both since they would be almost two days drive apart for the next six months until June 1969. Christmas day 1968 ended with a huge dinner in the main dining room and everything just seemed so right as Faith could now see her new family and her future right in front of her. She turned to Duke at the dinner table and said, "Why don't we get married New Year's Eve, I just can't stand the idea of being separated for the next six months and then being separated again for a year if they send you to Vietnam."

Duke smiled and said, "Pretty Lady, I will marry you tonight if you like?" They hugged each other and then Duke announced to everyone in the dining room that they were going to be married New Year's Eve! Faith called her parents right after supper and told them of their plans, and that they wanted them to drive to the ranch near Odessa the very next weekend. Everything went into high gear and Duke went the next day to the local courthouse to get a marriage license. Because of the Christmas holidays, Rodger Gabriel eventually had to pull in a few favors from the local county clerk to issue the license.

Everything was finally in place and the wedding took place New Year's Eve in the main barn at the Double Star Ranch. Faith wore a beautiful plain white western calico dress, that, while not a true wedding dress per-se, it was still absolutely beautiful. Adam Duke Gabriel wore dark western trousers, a black western sports coat, and western silver bolo tie.

He wore his very best solid Silver Belt Buckle that he had won in completion several years ago as a bronco rider in college. He topped it all off with a brand new Stetson western black felt hat that his father had bought for him especially for the wedding. Faith's bouquet was made from Texas wildflowers which she just dearly loved as it reminded her of her horse.

Faith's two sisters, Hope and Charity were her bridesmaids and Adam's Father, Roger Gabriel, and Faith's brother, Alex Anderson, stood up with Duke. The local church pastor was more than pleased to come to the ranch and perform the ceremony. The entire ceremony came together quite well and it looked like it had been planned that way for months instead of just days.

The couple took no honeymoon away from the ranch, opting to stay in the guest cabin, which by now had become quite comfortable for them both. Dorothy Gabriel stocked the cabin refrigerator with food and the newlyweds did not come up for air for the next three days.

When the newlyweds finally did leave the ranch cabin, it was only to go over to the main house to have supper with the combined families that were still staying at the ranch after the quickly planned wedding. Alex was perhaps the happiest member of the extended family, as he had been taking advantage of the ranch time to ride almost everywhere on the ranch on horseback. He had already planned to return during the upcoming summer for a summer ranch hand position as promised by Hobbs.

Duke spent a lot of time on the phone the next week trying to determine if there were any furnished apartments available in the Columbus, Georgia area for the newlyweds to set up their first household. He was not very successful and they finally decided that Faith should return back to San Angelo with her family. Faith would then give her two-week notice to her hospital and then join Duke at Fort Benning while Duke tried to solve the housing dilemma. Duke would go to Fort Benning and look for a place for them to live after he signed into his new unit of assignment.

Faith had given her two-week notice to the San Angelo Hospital upon returning to work after the Christmas Holiday. Her supervisors were very disappointed, as they really liked Faith, and saw great potential for her in their hospital. Faith's nursing degree and certification proved to be a real asset. She could almost always find new employment in almost any city, as nurses were in great demand almost everywhere. She decided to put her plans to join the Army Reserve on hold, as she just did not yet know how long they would be in Columbus, Georgia.

The move to Fort Benning was actually pretty uneventful. Duke rented a small U-Haul trailer for his pickup truck and hauled their few possessions and furniture. Faith had an antique dresser and mirror that she wanted to use in their master bedroom and Duke had a western trunk and several chairs that he had collected over the years that he liked. They would have to buy a bed and small dining table and chairs but they decided to wait until they knew better what they might need and whether they might qualify for army quarters on the fort. Duke drove the trailer to San Angelo and picked up Faith's furniture and clothing items and then started the trek to Fort Benning, Georgia.

If they somehow qualified for possible army quarters, Duke had been told by the housing office that the army usually provided some furniture items that might be available at the housing warehouse. It would all depend on when they became eligible and what might be available in the army-housing warehouse at that time.

Duke was already on the promotion list for First Lieutenant but would not be actually promoted until the anniversary date of his commissioning in June 1969. It was important for him to report to Fort Benning as quickly as possible after the New Year's Holiday, as his sign in date at Fort Benning would determine where he would be placed on the priority list for available housing on the Fort.

On post housing was somewhat limited for junior officers and many young lieutenants would have to live off post if they were not senior enough in rank to draw quarters on post. Single officers were easy to house in one of the several high-rise apartment buildings located on post. Married officers quarters were much more difficult to acquire, as most married couples had children and needed several bedrooms.

Duke and Faith were lucky. They had no children and they did not require much space and the smaller quarters were usually the last ones to be selected by married officers. Duke had rented the U-Haul trailer for a month and he was allowed to park the trailer in the Officers Club extended parking lot on the army post until he needed to unload it and return it to the local U-Haul dealer in the town of Columbus, Georgia.

Duke signed into post headquarters on 9 January 1969. Most new officers would not arrive at Fort Benning until the next week, which gave Duke and

Faith almost 6-7 days of priority status on the housing list. He was happy to find out that he would be offered quarters in Custer Terrace and he immediately drove out to the area on the post to check out the offered housing. Faith would not be coming to Fort Benning for another week as she was still working off her two-week notice at the hospital in San Angelo, Texas.

Duke immediately accepted the quarters offered by the army and set forth unloading the U-Haul trailer and cleaning the quarters so that they would look nice when Faith finally arrived next week sometime. In truth, he would have almost accepted a tent if offered, as he really wanted to be on post where proximity to his job would be a real plus in driving time everyday. The house was a standard ranch style home of about 1200 square feet with two small bedrooms and a large open family room/dining room combination and a small kitchen. It had only one bathroom, but it was a reasonable size and would work just fine for the couple.

He was not about to turn down the quarters as they might never be offered another set before all the other new officers arrived on post. He was so very pleased to have been offered the house and called Faith almost right away to give her the great news that they had a house on post.

Duke was assigned to be the Executive Officer of the Fort Benning Student Company, which meant that he would be responsible for much of the administrative duties of the Student Company at Fort Benning. It was a big job in that Fort Benning had hundreds of students coming and going all the time who needed to be processed into various training classes and their administrative needs were to be met by the student company cadre.

Duke equated the duties as much like those on the ranch. After all, you were herding students much like you herded cattle on the ranch, ensuring they were in the right place at the right time. Except that unlike cattle, these army students all had minds of their own and often did not easily comply with instructions.

He had to laugh at some of the dumb stunts students could play. Most new lieutenants were just now finally on their own in life and some had not yet learned the hard lessons of good individual responsibility when it came to drinking at night and being on time in the morning for the many formations required by the US Army.

Duke began to think that he was 'herding cats'! But everything eventually fell into place, and Duke got into a pretty good daily routine during his first week of assignment to the student company cadre. Faith arrived as planned the next week and she was actually quite pleased with the small set of quarters to which they had been assigned.

Faith immediately took 'possession' of the house and began turning it into a home with many very important feminine touches. By the end of their first month of marriage together, they were functioning well as a married couple and had firmly established a home on Fort Benning together.

Faith then turned her attention to finding a nursing job. She applied to the Martin Army Hospital on Fort Benning and at two hospitals in town. She was almost immediately offered employment at all three facilities. She finally decided to accept the offer at Martin Army Hospital because it was only four miles from their quarters and on nice days, she could actually ride her bicycle there.

Duke was assigned to the student company as the executive officer, but spent only one month in the job, because he was soon noticed by the Deputy Commanding General of Fort Benning and quickly selected to be the General's aide-de-camp. The new job was very demanding and kept him on the post many hours every day. By the first of March 1969, both he and Faith were highly involved in their positions at Fort Benning.

Their relationship and marriage blossomed and Duke and Faith were so much in love that they were noticed everywhere they went together because of the obvious love they had for one another. Faith was so glad that she had insisted on them getting married over the Christmas Holidays, as she could not have stood the separation that Duke's assignment to Fort Benning would have brought. This was especially true once Duke was selected to be the General's aide and had little 'extra' time to travel anywhere.

The next five months went by in a blur. Before either Faith or Duke realized it, The July Fourth Holiday came and went. Duke received his orders for Vietnam right after the holiday. The couple sat down and started planning the next year. Should Faith stay at Fort Benning or return home to San Angelo to be closer to extended family? It was a big decision.

Faith had grown to love her job at Martin Army Hospital and had made several close friends at the hospital. She was also still considering joining the Army Reserve in Columbus, Georgia, and a move back to San Angelo would mean seeking a new job, or trying to fit back into her family's store and farm. She finally decided to stay at Fort Benning, as she really liked their army quarters and did not want the hassle of another move.

The next several weeks were spent getting Duke ready to leave for Vietnam. It was a sad time for the couple and Faith took it upon herself to make the separation the best situation that could be by putting together a small photo album for Duke to take with him to Vietnam. She vowed to write him as often as possible and reminded him to send his address as soon as he knew what unit and where he would be assigned in Vietnam.

In Faith's mind, the army was all screwed up on their assignment polices to Vietnam. No one ever knew in advance just what unit they were to be assigned to in Vietnam and would not know until they actually arrived there. That seemed just plain dumb to Faith? But to Duke, it just reinforced in his mind that the army needed all the good leaders they could find to overcome such obstacles. He promised to write Faith as soon as he knew where he would be located.

Faith saw Duke to the airport in Columbus and said a tearful goodbye inside the main terminal. Both sets of parents had made the trip to Fort Benning to say goodbye to Duke Gabriel. Duke was to fly first to Seattle, Washington and then on to Hawaii and then to Vietnam. He would be in the air many hours and would arrive there probably exhausted.

He kissed Faith goodbye and told her not to worry because, after all, he was an army ranger! He hugged his parents and his in laws and said goodbye to everyone. Duke took Alex off to the side and told him to keep an eye on his big sister, as she might need him if Duke was injured or killed in Vietnam. It was really more than Alex could process but he promised to be there for his sister if needed. Duke then walked out to the plane and took off into the summer sky.

Chapter Eleven: Day Five Alone
4 April 1970

Duke was very sore. No matter what he tried to do, everything seemed to hurt even more. As if his left knee wasn't giving him enough problems, now his right knee and leg were also both now hurting. This was probably because he was favoring his right leg trying to keep weight off the left knee. He was in bad shape. He had never hurt like this before. Even when he played football, a good soak in a tub would repair almost any injury. He doubted he would ever be the same again. He also had started having headaches.

He had painfully discovered that explosive and blast injuries were a different kind of injury completely from other lesser injuries he had sustained in the past. For the first time, he was feeling older than his age and wondered if he could survive this ordeal if the enemy were to come after them in his current reduced capacity. He now knew what a wounded animal felt when the hunter was on his trail and he was hurting. He had to wonder if he and Tim could survive this ordeal. Ranger school had thrown him many scenarios to consider, but nothing like this.

The only self-defense weapons they had were three knives, his pistol, and several grenades they had found in some of the rucksacks they had hidden. But even throwing a grenade when seated on the ground would be difficult. Hand grenades were usually thrown while standing up, because you could put the full force of your arm, chest, and torso behind each throw. Throwing a grenade while seated on the ground was a much more difficult operation. Add that every muscle in his body was screaming sore already, would make the act almost impossible. But to stand up to throw, would make him such a good target, that he would probably be shot to death easily.

Duke's mind was beginning to play tricks on him and the lack of substantial amounts of real food was beginning to take a toll on both of their stamina's. Duke began to fear that he could actually hallucinate and that it could be fatal if he mistook a hallucination to be a real scenario. He had been purposely eating as little as possible in an attempt to save the cans of rations they had left. Now he was second-guessing that decision.

Duke figured they could hold out for a month that way but he now wondered if their bodies could hold out as long as he thought their minds would. They both consumed large amounts of water, as it was readily available from the many streams and rains in the area.

Duke had just completed digging their second small toilet off from their location by crisscrossing branches over a hole he had dug, as Tim could not possibly squat over a simple hole. Tim had to be able to sit and the crisscrossed branches did the trick, as Tim could slide onto the branches to support his weight. Duke then used the same entrenching tool they had found on the LZ to throw dirt in the hole every day over the waste to prevent any smells that might give away their location. Survival was a lot harder out here in the real jungle than when he had studied the problems in an army classroom.

He found it hard to believe that the battalion had not come back to the LZ since the day of the mortar attack. Surely they knew by now that Tim and Duke were not among the dead? If that were true, why had they not returned to search for them? Something was terribly wrong?

At that very moment, back at the 85th Army Hospital Morgue on Camp Eagle, a young medic was completing a listing of bodies and their matching names that had been identified from the combat action on LZ 'Saber,' the name now given to the LZ on Hill 786, involving the First Platoon of D Company, 1/327th Battalion on 30 March 1970.

The medical sergeant finished his report and then placed the documents into an envelope for filing. He was late for a formation and inadvertently missed the fact that the names of the missing from that action had actually continued onto another sheet of paper stuck to the first sheet. Those two missing soldiers on page two were Corporal Tim Turner and First Lieutenant Adam Duke Gabriel.

Because the sergeant had missed seeing the second page of the battalion report, the fact that no bodies had matched the remaining two soldiers names went unnoticed. The file was placed into a letter storage bin and the world went on without notification to any higher authority that the two additional soldiers were still actually missing in action and that no body parts for Corporal Turner or Lieutenant Gabriel had been yet recovered from the LZ.

The battalion commander of the 1/327th had filled out missing in action, presumed dead, reports on all of the soldiers from the LZ. The names included Corporal Turner, Lieutenant Gabriel, along with six other soldiers that made up the Fourth Squad of 1st Platoon, D Company, 1/327th Infantry and four Warrant Officers that had been the pilots. The report that had been submitted on March 31st, 1970 totaled twelve soldiers. His action had started the notification procedures for all of the combatants that were presumed killed that day.

Corporal Turner had been blown off the same LZ as had Duke and had landed very close to the lieutenant. That left both Duke and Tim alive, but at the moment, unfortunately, no one in their battalion knew they were still alive, and that they were continuing to try to survive alone together in the jungle just north of Firebase Veghel.

Duke started to think that no one might ever come to save them and they might have to try and grow stronger and eventually walk their way out of the jungle toward Firebase Veghel. But that could take weeks, and could they find enough food to survive such an ordeal? Just as he was thinking those thoughts he heard yelling and voices from the LZ on hilltop #786. Unfortunately, the voices he heard were speaking in Vietnamese and were not their friends but rather their enemy.

Duke immediately woke Tim up and told him to be quiet by placing a finger against Tim's lips. Tim came to full alert and reached for the grenade he kept close to his body. The enemy had finally returned to the LZ to assess the damages. Duke had known in his gut that they would eventually return and sure enough, here they were. Duke moved a little closer to the trail so he could get a look down off the hill where they were currently hiding. He saw probably ten to twenty NVA soldiers walking all around the LZ and in the jungle just off of the LZ.

He held his breath as the soldiers took their time walking all around the LZ and looking at the burned and charred debris left by the two helicopters. Duke hoped that they would not start looking around the LZ and into the thick underbrush where he had hidden the last two caches of supplies. He had moved three of the rucksacks closer to their current position yesterday but the heavy rains of the past two days had prevented him from returning to move the other two caches that he still had hidden in the thick brush just off the LZ.

The enemy soldiers spent about an hour looking around the LZ and they evidently took something out of each of the destroyed helicopters before moving off. They went back up the trail the way they had come into the LZ. That was a relief, as they were not going to pass right by their current positions.

But this demonstrated that the enemy was still in this area and that any movement had to be undertaken with extreme care so as not to make excessive noise. He had returned to their hiding spot and had just gotten himself comfortable again when Tim tapped him on the shoulder with the long stick that he used to communicate silently. Tim put his finger to his lips indicating silence and then pointed to his ears like he had heard something. Since Duke's ears were still ringing from the explosions, his hearing was not quite as good as it normally was.

Duke immediately began to listen in earnest and then he heard the sounds too. Someone was coming up the trail from the LZ. Duke pulled his 45caliber pistol but he sincerely hoped that he would not have to use it, as the sound would undoubtedly bring back the enemy platoon they had just seen on the LZ. They lay low in the jungle grass as the sound got closer and closer. Eventually, two men passed right by their position headed south toward the villages. They appeared to be very young and did not appear to be armed.

They were evidently some kind of couriers or messengers from the NVA and they were headed toward the villages in the valley below. Duke assumed that they must be members of the local Viet Cong, (VC) and that they were the middlemen in the operation of the VC with the NVA currently in the area. He had known that some villages evidently were periodically communicating with the NVA Army hidden in the jungle, but this was the first time he had seen the operation actually taking place right in front of him. He would have to report the activity to his superiors when they got back. Then he thought, "If they ever got back."

Duke again thought about Psalm 40 that had promised him a safe place. He found it comforting that he was thinking about the Lord and he then shared his thoughts with Tim as they lay there in the grass. He told Tim to have faith, as he was absolutely sure that the Lord was with them and had purposely saved them. Tim had never accepted Jesus into his life because of the miserable home in which he was raised. He now thought that he should look into religion a bit more since the LT was so sure that God had saved them. Tim had not trusted his own father, but he trusted Duke with his life. If Duke believed in God, then Tim was ready to accept God into his own life. Duke assured Tim that there were few nonbelievers in combat.

At that same moment back at the 85th Evacuation Hospital, LT Faith Gabriel was going about her daily routine when one of the sergeants came into the clinic from the morgue. He mentioned that he had heard that she was married to one of the missing soldiers of the 327th infantry. He told her that he had been part of the team that had identified the ten men killed on LZ 786 and that he was sorry for her loss. She thanked the young sergeant for his concern and went on with her daily routine.

She finally got a break later in the afternoon and as she got off her shift, she made her way back to the female nurse barracks where she had her bunk. She was not senior enough in rank to get her own room so she was currently rooming with two other young nurses. They fell into a comfortable conversation about their day and then went to supper together to the mess tent just down the road.

She returned to their room and decided to write a letter to her mother about her work and the terrible loss of Duke and his platoon members. Something was bothering her but she could not put a finger on it, as she got her paper out and laid out her writing materials. She started doodling on a sheet of paper and then it hit her as she was doodling. The young sergeant from the morgue had told her he felt sorry for the loss of the ten men identified from the LZ? Ten soldiers, that's what had bothered her? She had done the math on her own and had come up with twelve total soldiers from the LZ explosions, not ten?

She took the pad of paper out and started to jot down what she had known to be true: there were six squad members in the fourth squad of First Platoon. Then there were four helicopter pilots, two in each bird, which brought the total up to ten. Finally, there was Duke and Tim, his RTO, which then brought the total to twelve, but only eight soldiers of the twelve had belonged to Duke's battalion. That's what was bothering her earlier this afternoon; the sergeant had clearly said, ten total soldiers, not twelve? Why?

She continued with her plan to write her mother and finished her letter. She would have to go over to the morgue tomorrow and find that young sergeant. She wanted to challenge his memory about the number of soldiers missing from Duke's battalion. It was probably just a counting error, but it still bothered her that he had clearly said ten and not twelve men?

Could there have been a mistake in the count? And if so, could two soldiers actually be missing as opposed to dead? She knew that simple mistakes happened every day in the hospital, but they had never lost two bodies before, or at least she thought they had never lost anyone? She would explore the dilemma tomorrow when she was better rested and thinking a bit clearer. Right now she was too tired to think about it all. She had to get to bed and get some rest or she would be of little help tomorrow in the clinic.

Back on the hilltop in the jungle, Duke was once again taking inventory of their equipment and planning what he would do if they had to leave in a hurry. He had packed everything tightly into two rucksacks he had brought to their location. Just before dusk he had ventured back the LZ on hill 786, retrieved the other two caches buried there in the brush and moved them to a new hiding place halfway up the hill to their current location, where they would be easier to get to when needed.

As darkness fell over the jungle he returned to the hiding spot and found Tim asleep. But something was wrong. Tim's breathing sounded labored and he was even coughing a little bit. Duke put his head next to Tim's chest and could hear the raspy sound of his lungs. Tim had a cold or was coming down with the flu, either of which could prove extremely dangerous out here in the jungle.

They had no cold or flu medicine out here and if it was actually the flu, it could prove fatal for Tim in his already deteriorated state. Duke began to worry that things could actually get much worse for Tim. That night he again wrapped Tim well in the two poncho liners using his own added to Tim's. He had to keep Tim warm.

Chapter Twelve: Fort Benning and Vietnam

Seven months earlier

September 1969

Faith Gabriel came home to their assigned quarters at Fort Benning and found the latest letter from her husband Duke, presently serving in Vietnam, in their mailbox. She sat down with a glass of iced tea and opened the letter and began to read:

Dearest Faith:

Well, I have finally made it to my unit of assignment, so the return address on this envelope is the address to which you can now write to me. I am the First Platoon Leader of D Company, 1/327th Infantry. My platoon consists of only eighteen soldiers right now.

The unit just came off duty in the Ashau Valley where it had taken losses of over twelve people wounded or killed. When the company lost two of its three platoon leaders, they sent the company back to Firebase Bastogne to await replacements.

It's a great little platoon of young soldiers. It is obvious that they have already seen a lot of action as they have the shell-shocked look of soldiers who have been stretched to their endurance point. It will take me a few days to get their morale back to normal but all in all, they seem to be a good bunch of guys.

My Platoon Sergeant is an experienced senior NCO named Sergeant First Class (SFC) Travis Bell. He is from Oklahoma, so I already feel close to him since we are from the same part of the country.

It's obviously going to be a long year over here as the war is constant and the workday is twenty-four hours long, not twelve hours long, as back at Benning. Even when I sleep, it is very lightly since anything can happen at any moment. I just wanted to get my new address to you quickly so please forgive the short length of this letter, as I must get back to my duties.

I love you darling and already miss you so very much. I keep a photo of you attached to my map that I carry every day in my shirt to remind me of you and home. Stay with me honey, as I think of you often, and write when you get the chance. Mail is very important to everyone over here and is delivered with every resupply chopper that comes to the platoon. We get resupply birds almost every week so we look forward to the birds and the mailbag.

I hope all is well there? Please call my folks and pass on the new address. All my Love, Always, Adam.

Faith put down the letter and thought about Duke and the danger he now faced daily in Vietnam. Duke had only been gone a little over three weeks, and already Faith was beginning to think that her present housing arrangement would make her extremely lonely for the next year. She had to start thinking about other possibilities and opportunities that might be open to her. Her husband was serving his country in Vietnam for the next year. How could she likewise serve her country and also be closer to her husband?

Thoughts began to take root. Maybe it was time for her to put into motion ideas she had been tossing around for over two years now? After all, she was a nurse, the army needed nurses, and she had no children to care for and was much more free to move than many other wives and nurses.

The next week found Duke Gabriel also thinking about his current situation and his assignment to the 101st Airborne Airmobile Division. He had mixed emotions today. Today was the one-month anniversary of his combat tour in Vietnam. It was hard to believe that he had been here for a month already.

Time sure flew in the war. In fact, one month was almost a nonexistent measure of his war experience. Time was hourly, not monthly in nature in Vietnam. There just seemed to be no day or night as everything just ran together. Each day was twenty-four hours long and often sleep was taken only when it was safe to do so.

He was leading a great platoon of eighteen very young and yet tough little soldiers. Duke and his platoon sergeant were the only two men over twenty-one years old. Duke was twenty-three and his platoon sergeant, Sergeant First Class (SFC) Travis Bell was the oldest in the platoon at thirty-two years old. Almost all the rest of the platoon soldiers were under twenty years of age, the one exception being his first squad leader, Buck Sergeant (E5) Roger Burns, who would turn twenty-one in the next week.

Duke was really in his element as a platoon leader in the 101st Airborne Division. A cowboy at heart and fact, 'raised' on a ranch south of Odessa, Texas, Duke took to the leadership challenge like a fish to water. He did not plan to make the army a career, but in his family, a man had to serve his country or he just wasn't a man at all. His father and grandfather had both been infantrymen and by God, he was not going to be outdone.

He had accepted an ROTC scholarship at the University Of Texas in Austin while in college and then accepted an active duty commission when it was offered which automatically assured he would be going to Vietnam to serve his country. He volunteered for every training course offered by the army and had completed both Airborne and Ranger training before being assigned to Vietnam.

Of course, at the time he had accepted the scholarship and army commitment he had not been married to Faith Anderson and the call to arms just seemed the right thing to do. Now that he had a wife, the war in Vietnam was something that he just had to survive. He could then return to the love of his life, one Faith Anderson, now Mrs. Adam 'Duke' Gabriel.

Adam was Duke's given name, but everyone in the army just called him "Duke", which was actually his middle name given to him by his father, an unabashed fan of John Wayne. His mother insisted on the name Adam because he was their firstborn. She was a very Christian woman and while she did not always make it to church, she read the bible daily.

Life on a working cattle ranch left little time for church, as Sundays were the only rest day of the week, and the nearest church was almost an hour away. But Duke's mother insured that her children would know the Lord, and made them study the bible every Sunday at the ranch. Duke had grown up on that family ranch in Texas and few in town actually knew his first name. He was known by almost everyone as "Duke". Even his cowboy boots and saddle had the name etched in the leather.

Duke had tried hard to live up to his father's expectations and had become an accomplished cowboy, cattleman, and wrangler. Ranching was in his blood and he planned to return to the ranch once his education and service obligation were complete. Of course, he had not planned on meeting Faith Anderson at graduation which would change his life forever, but that was another story. Right now, surviving his Vietnam tour and going home to Faith, were the only things on his mind if he wanted to stay alive and keep his platoon safe.

He and his platoon sergeant, SFC Travis Bell were both busy planning their first actual platoon insertion together into the jungle of Vietnam. Because the platoon had a new platoon leader, the battalion leaders had been using the platoon for firebase security until they felt that Duke got his bearings as a platoon leader.

Platoons in Vietnam were used as Firebase Security and to search for and destroy the enemy. His platoon had been securing the wire perimeter of the firebase for the last week. His Company Commander had decided that it was now time to put Duke and his platoon further into the jungle from the firebase using helicopters of the 101st Aviation Brigade to pick them up at the firebase.

Duke would meet his company commander, Captain Barclay, on the first helicopter (bird) that came to pick up the platoon. He and the company commander would then have a few minutes to talk before Duke's platoon was inserted into the new area of operations. Duke would get a map from Captain Barclay and then secure the landing zone (LZ) with his first squad, which would be inserted with the platoon leader.

It was a procedure that would become constant when the platoon was moved from a secure LZ to an insecure LZ in any new area. The platoon leader would take the first bird in and the platoon sergeant would come in on the last bird. This made sure there was leadership with the platoon at all times.

Extractions from enemy territory were usually done in the opposite, the platoon sergeant going out first and the platoon leader coming out last. The hair on Duke's arm suddenly stood up as he awaited the birds, a reaction that Duke always recognized as one of danger or alert that happened to him every time he sensed danger or anticipation. He sensed that this new area did, in fact, pose an extreme danger to his platoon.

The standard operating procedure (SOP) of the platoon leader going in the first helicopter was company policy used on every insertion into known enemy territory the platoon made. Duke talked with his company commander and Captain Barclay then gave

Duke a new map as expected. The map had some rally points already marked and coded by number on the sheet, which the two men could use for reference during this upcoming operation when they talked daily over the radio.

Once on the ground, Duke immediately moved his platoon away from the LZ and into the thicker jungle. This protected the platoon from any possible enemy mortar fire that might be brought because of all the noise and activity of the helicopters. Once away from the LZ, Duke contacted Captain Barclay and told him that all was secure and that the platoon was safely off the LZ.

The platoon then formed a security perimeter inside the jungle about 300 meters from the LZ. They took a lunch break and Duke's Radio Telephone Operator, (RTO), Corporal Tim Turner, opened the mailbag they had just been given on the helicopter, and began passing out mail. Corporal Tim Turner had only been the platoon RTO for the past week. Duke had selected Tim when the old RTO had finished his tour of duty in Vietnam and had left the platoon headed back to the states.

SFC Bell told Duke that Duke should choose his own RTO, as the sergeant knew that Duke would probably be with his RTO for the next year in Vietnam. The RTO and the Platoon leader had to work daily together and SFC Bell knew it would be better if Duke had someone close to him daily that he trusted and liked.

Duke had easily chosen Tim Turner to be his RTO. He had been watching all of the soldiers intently over the past month and he had already formed several opinions on their personalities, strengths and apparent weaknesses. Duke had noticed Tim Turner early on in his tour as being introverted and quiet. But he liked the young man, as he appeared to be quite competent and always followed instructions well.

Tim was not boastful; he refrained from telling war stories, and generally acted like a young man with a purpose. Duke thought that Tim was carrying a burden of some type. He was obviously very young, so Duke wondered if he had been drafted or if he had volunteered? He was a little bit of a mystery to Duke, but Duke trusted the young soldier. He just liked the young man.

As Tim continued to sort the mail that had been just given to the platoon, he turned towards Duke and handed him a letter from the stack sitting in front of Corporal Turner. Duke had just received his first letter from his wife from that mailbag. He had sent her his address once he got his unit of assignment, but the mail took almost seven to ten days one way from the states, so he had not received any mail until today.

Duke thanked his RTO for the letter, and Tim just smiled and said, "It smells good LT, so it must be from your wife?" Duke sat down with his back to a tree and opened the letter carefully as if it were made of glass.

My Dearest Adam:

I miss you already more than I can say, darling. I just don't think I can sit here in these army quarters at Fort Benning for a full year without your presence. My new job in the emergency room of Martin Army Hospital gives me something to do, but I miss our evenings together and worry about you daily.

I have decided to join the Army Reserve Nursing Program as we had talked about before you left the states. I just cannot sit here for the next year worrying about you when I can do something productive and perhaps be able to see you once or twice if I volunteer for a six month Temporary Duty (TDY) assignment at a hospital hopefully close to the 101st Division in Vietnam.

They need emergency room qualified nurses and I fit the bill perfectly. There are temporary duty positions open in Phu Bai, Vietnam, which looks to be quite close to the 101st Airborne. I hope you do not mind my volunteering, but I just have to be closer to you if I can get there and I would probably finish my six-month tour and be back home here and working again at Martin Army Hospital at Fort Benning before your tour would end next August.

I plan to leave here next week for San Antonio Texas for a three-week orientation school where I will be appointed a First Lieutenant by direct commission in the Army Reserve Nurse Corps. There is a special program just for qualified nurses that grant direct commissions and six-month tours with no other reserve duty requirement after we return. They are desperate for nurses and are offering all kinds of temporary programs and options to attract nurses. Martin Army Hospital must hold my job position by law, while I am serving on active duty.

I have enclosed a slip of paper with my new unit address in San Antonio so that you can write to me there. Then hopefully, I will be in Phu Bai by the end of October.

I love you so much my darling and I hope you agree with my decision. I just have to do something and I am so very qualified for the Army's needs right now. I will be safe at the hospital and perhaps you might actually be able to see me once or twice while I am there. Wouldn't that be great?

I called both sets of parents and told them of my decision, and they are supportive, but of course, they are also worried.

I must close as I have a lot to do to get ready for my flight to San Antonio to the Army Nurse Corps Orientation School. The Fort Benning Housing Office has agreed to hold our quarters while I am gone, and our neighbor Captain Joe Munson will check the house periodically. I will return by the end of May, so I will not have to move any of our furniture and belongings and I will have a home to come back to after my tour obligation.

I must close now and get some sleep as I have a very big day ahead of me tomorrow. Wish me luck! All My love, Faith

Duke laid the letter in his lap and thought of Faith and the letter he had just read. It was just like her to volunteer as an Army Nurse. She too had a strong desire to serve her country and he could not fault her thinking, but it did mean he would worry about her safety. It would also mean that he would probably get even fewer letters from her in the future. Darn!

He got up and headed toward SFC Bell, as they needed to get the platoon moving toward their night ambush site before dark. He had instructions from Captain Barclay to set out an 'L shaped' ambush on a highly used trail thought to be the main supply route out of the mountains heading to the villages east of the Firebase.

He briefed all of the squad leaders and then sent them back to their squads to plan for the night ambush. SFC Bell stayed with Duke for a few more minutes and they discussed the upcoming ambush and just what they expected tonight. SFC Bell felt much the same as his LT, that this new area had enemy soldiers present, as he had noticed well-used trails in this new area. It was obvious that someone was using the trails here to travel back and forth from the villages in the valley below.

That night at almost 3AM (0300 Hrs.) two enemy squads walked down the well-traveled trail and right into the ambush set up by the First Platoon. Duke started the ambush by firing his own M-16, one of the few times he ever fired his own weapon. Everyone engaged the enemy target and bullets flew for the next ten minutes in all directions.

When the smoke cleared, 15 enemy soldiers were dead, two were wounded badly and thankfully, no one in Duke's platoon had sustained any injuries. It was just the type of action that the platoon needed to bolster its own confidence again. The losses in the Ashau Valley were quickly forgotten and the new First Platoon was on a roll!

Chapter Thirteen: Day Six Alone
5 April 1970

Duke and Tim had been lying low since yesterday afternoon when the enemy soldiers had arrived to search the abandoned LZ and when the two couriers had passed by their hiding position. It had taken the enemy longer to arrive back on Hill 786 than Duke had originally estimated, but it was clear the enemy soldiers were aware of what had happened there and they were just now searching for any weapons or booty that might be harvested or confiscated from the LZ.

Duke now wondered if his new caches were hidden well enough and if they were safe here on the next hilltop, or if any of their footprints might lead the enemy to their location. He had tried diligently to erase any evidence of their direction of movement but he wondered if he had done enough to fool the enemy soldiers. If they found any of the caches, they would know that someone was left alive and that could lead to their complete discovery.

Duke and Tim had sat very still all afternoon the previous day trying not to make any noise whatsoever that might disclose their location. He had barely been able to sleep last night and was extremely hungry and thirsty. He badly wanted to move but felt that any movement could compromise their location. He did not want to go to get food from one of his three caches because the hidden food was still too close to the LZ. Tim's cold seemed to have improved overnight and he was a bit better today.

Duke now wished he had hidden the food further from the LZ, but at the time he was in so much pain that he just could not carry the C-ration loaded rucksacks very far before hiding them in the jungle. His intention at the time was to get as many cans of food hidden in a cache as quickly as possible and to get he and Tim off of the LZ before the enemy discovered them.

Because Duke had initially hidden the food even closer to the LZ than they were now, there remained some empty holes around the LZ that might signal to the enemy that someone had been digging in the area. Duke did not dare to return to the LZ and just hoped the recent rains had camouflaged and filled in the holes that he had left uncovered.

He now knew that his actions of moving the caches had been prudent indeed, as the enemy had come after all and did look around the LZ. The enemy soldiers had stayed around the LZ for over an hour and had finally left the hilltop going back north on the paths they had come down just a few hours before. They had evidently quelled their curiosity and decided to go back to wherever they were staying in the area. Thank God they had not discovered any of his hidden caches.

Duke was very glad he had decided to seek shelter on the next hilltop to the south, closer to Firebase Veghel. Now he wondered how long he should wait before attempting to get to one of his two remaining caches just down the hill from their current location. He also wondered if the enemy had left anyone behind to ambush anyone who might be in the area?

Duke had failed to count the soldiers he saw at the LZ yesterday. Had he actually counted the number of soldiers, it might have given him some idea if a few soldiers had been left behind when they finally left. He was now kicking himself for his lack of attention to detail. He knew that his mind was not as sharp as it had been before the explosions. He worried that he might be deteriorating mentally almost daily.

Duke decided to wait another day before trying to get to their remaining food caches. They would have to just eat a couple of more bananas and make due, as returning towards the LZ right now was just too dangerous. His biggest concerns today were the burns on his arms, legs and torso and Tim's leg pain, which was still rather intense and Tim's burns and apparent cold or flu. He was beginning to wonder if perhaps Tim had some internal bleeding which could prove fatal to the young man.

Every burn on Duke's body hurt and he wondered if he should try to use any leaves or roots to perhaps ease his pain. He knew that some leaves like Aloe Vera leaves could be used to soothe burns, but he did not really know what such leaves looked like, or if they even grew in the jungles of Vietnam at all?

He again mentally chastised himself for not better preparing for his tour in Vietnam. He should have researched what plants might be medically beneficial before he ever came to Vietnam. He remembered an instructor in Ranger School mentioning that you could test leaves for edibility by tasting them with your tongue and if they were bitter, not to eat them. But he now wondered if that was really true.

Duke also remembered that someone else had once told him that leaves that contained a gel-like substance might ease the pain when rubbed on a rash or injury. But he had absolutely no idea which leaves might be good for burns, or which might just add to the already burning pain? He finally decided that he would try a couple different leaves on the burns on his arm and see what developed. He felt he had nothing to lose, as his pain level was so high that he feared passing out.

He spent the rest of the day looking for possible jungle leaves and experimenting with each one to see if any might give any relief to his burns. He was so very hungry, yet he dared not return to get any more of the C-ration cans until he knew for sure that the LZ was empty of any additional enemy soldiers. He was also so very weak, as was Tim, that he doubted his ability to protect them should any enemy soldier confront them right now.

As if things weren't bad enough, that afternoon he was trying to get comfortable at the base of the tree where he was hiding, when he placed his hand unintentionally on a snake that was lying in the grass and was bitten on the side of his left hand. He quickly pulled his hand back as the small snake made a quick exit and wondered if the snake was poisonous or even perhaps fatal.

An hour later he had his answer. His hand had swelled almost twice its size and he was feeling numb and disoriented. Obviously, the snake had been poisonous to some degree. He had cut his hand with his knife between the fang marks and tried to squeeze the venom out of his hand. He had seen many TV cowboy actors do such cutting in movie scenes as he had grown up. He hoped they were correct?

He did not use his mouth to suck out the venom because his lips were still split and they would only give the venom another entry point to his body even closer to his brain. Tim had then surprisingly taken charge and tried to squeeze more of the venom out of Duke's Hand.

Duke fell asleep, and Tim continued to administer to the young lieutenant by his side.

Tim was actually glad to have something to do, as it took his mind off of his own rather severe injuries. The next several hours were very tense as Tim tried to keep Duke awake, as he was afraid that if Duke fell into a coma, he would die. Tim put a tourniquet on Duke's arm above the bite and continued to try to squeeze the venom out of Duke's hand by massaging the hand and pushing clear liquid and blood out of the wound. It seemed like hours had passed, but both men no longer had much sense of time unless they actually looked at Duke's Rolex which his father had given him on graduation day.

Duke was a mess. He now wondered if his final moments might be upon him. He evidently then fell asleep and awoke later with a dry mouth and fever. But thankfully, the venom must have had the effect of numbing the pain from his burns. His hand still hurt and was still rather swelled, but his mind seemed clear and he had obviously not died. He smiled at Tim, who was leaning over him diligently trying to mitigate the damage done by the snake.

Duke almost laughed at himself at that point. How could things get much worse? Their unit had abandoned them, they were both hungry, he was snake bit, and he was miserable, so just what else could happen to make things any worse? He looked up at Tim and the sky beyond, wondering if it was now about to rain and make him even more miserable. That answer came immediately as the rain began to fall. What an unfriendly country this place was?

After an hour of continuous rain, he finally began to feel a bit better and had released the tourniquet that Tim had placed on his arm. Duke decided that either the actions he and Tim had taken were good, or perhaps the snake was not as venomous as they had feared as his head began to clear. He then decided that he would try and get to one of his food caches to get something to eat for them both. They were both very hungry.

The rain was so loud in the jungle that it might actually cover his movements and also erase his footprints. He was the only one of them that could possibly walk, so he had to get his ass up and try. He cautiously got up and began moving around to see if he could walk. To his surprise, he could actually walk without any dizziness. He told Tim to stay put and slowly began the trek back down the hill toward the LZ.

Tim tried to convince him to stay, as Tim was afraid that Duke might pass out and then die, as there was no way Tim could come to his rescue and Tim felt they had to stay together. Duke reassured the young Corporal that he was feeling much better and that they could not go much longer without solid food.

As Duke went down the hill and then climbed back up the other hill and approached the LZ holding his pistol, he was careful to look all around for any signs of any enemy soldiers. It appeared that no one had been left behind. He stopped often to just listen to the noises of the jungle but heard nothing that alarmed him.

He holstered the pistol and found his first Cache near the base of Hill 786 where he had hidden the rucksack. He decided to take the entire rucksack with him back to his hiding place on the next hill. He picked up the rucksack and then covered the hole where it had been hidden. It took him over an hour to get back up his hill and back to Tim's hiding spot in the trees at the top of the next hill. It had been raining the entire time and the hills were slippery and muddy, but the good news was that his footprints would soon be completely erased by the monsoon-like rain.

He then decided to move them both a bit further back from the trail into the dense jungle where they could fashion a very rudimentary lean-to using a poncho he had found in the cache, and covering it with branches to camouflage their hiding spot. He then settled back against a tree and opened a C-ration can of eggs and ham for each of them. It had never tasted better to him in his entire life. He had never had a better meal. He thanked God for the small ration can he was holding in his hands. Tim enjoyed his meal and again thanked the LT for everything he was doing for them.

Duke told Tim that they were now partners and that Tim had probably kept Duke alive after the snakebite incident. Tim smiled and said that he would never forget the LT and all that he was doing for them both. Tim then fell asleep as he had been awake for almost sixteen hours straight and badly need some sleep. Duke sat and thought of his wife, Faith, and whether he might ever see her again. He took out the map and her picture and looked at the photo for a long time. A lone tear ran down his face and he thought that she might never know of his survival and fight to get back to her again.

At that very moment in time, Faith Gabriel was assisting in surgery with a severely wounded young soldier. Out of no-where came a sense of anticipation, and the hair on her arms rose. She had never had such a sensation that she could remember, but she knew that the phenomenon was common for Duke, her husband. She actually looked around the operating room to see if something had happened to cause the strange reaction. She saw nothing that alarmed her.

As soon as the surgery ended and she had the next break, she began to think that God was perhaps trying to tell her something while she was in the operating room? It had been almost a week since the report of Duke's death. But something told her that she should investigate just what the forensics folks had discovered? The conversation earlier yesterday with the young sergeant over just how many soldiers had been identified came back into her mind. She had to go to the morgue and ask more questions. After all, she was at the very hospital where these folks worked in another section of the hospital. As soon as her shift was over, she started walking to the morgue.

Chapter Fourteen: Firebase Bastogne, Vietnam

Four Months Earlier
December 1969

Duke Gabriel was eating a C-ration meal with his Radio Telephone Operator (RTO) Corporal Tim Turner. Tim Turner had finally been promoted to Corporal from Specialist for being earlier selected to be Lieutenant Gabriel's RTO. Corporal stripes put him into the chain of command in the platoon and not just a regular soldier. The RTO position was considered a leadership position, so he had been given the two Corporal Stripes to replace his Specialist chevron. While he would get no more pay, he would get a lot more respect and he was quite proud of his two new new stripes.

RTO's were chosen by their platoon or company commanders based on many factors, the most important one being compatibility with the leader. The Platoon RTO served as the assistant to the Platoon leader and also carried many extra duties such as field clerk, mailman, and aide. In fact, the C-ration that Duke was now enjoying had just been heated by his RTO while the LT was planning operations with the company commander talking together on the radio.

Corporal Turner thought very highly of his platoon leader and saw his mission in life was to make the LT's job a bit easier if he could. He also thought of himself as the bodyguard for his LT, because the Lieutenant was often on the radio and not watching out for his own security. Lieutenants rarely pulled their personal pistol or shot their own M-16 rifle. They were too busy all of the time communicating on the radio with a myriad of support and command headquarters.

Duke finished his Radio conversation and his C-ration and thanked Corporal Turner for heating it, and then got onto his feet to check the perimeter of the platoon. Corporal Turner was busy sorting the mail they had just received on the resupply helicopter that had just visited the platoon an hour ago. The platoon had received their weekly resupply of clean fatigues, mail, ammunition, and food and had then moved from the LZ before stopping, setting up a security perimeter, and then having lunch.

The platoon had also received some new replacements and had now grown in size from just eighteen men when Duke had taken command, to their current size of twenty-seven. This allowed Duke and his platoon sergeant to form the fourth squad. Duke was now leading four squads of six men each and with his platoon headquarters element composed of Duke, SFC Bell, and Corporal Turner it brought the platoon total to twenty-seven soldiers.

Their present location was on a hilltop about 3000 meters from Firebase Bastogne. The Battalion headquarters was located on the firebase and the various companies of the battalion were arrayed around the mountainous area to the west of Bastogne. Everyone in the platoon was hoping that the Battalion would bring the companies back to Camp Eagle for Christmas. But no word had been sent out yet about the holiday and no one knew where the platoon might be on Christmas day.

There were several stories in the Stars and Stripes newspapers that had been delivered with the mail that day that several Hollywood entertainers were going to come to Camp Eagle for a Christmas Show. Every soldier in the entire 1st Brigade (Two Battalions) was hoping that they might get a stand down to watch the show. The 1/327th Battalion had not been to a USO show since last summer.

Obviously, not every unit would get to see the show, and they hoped that the 1/327th Infantry would be that battalion. Duke had asked his company commander about the possibility of a stand down and had been told that Captain Barclay knew nothing yet. Duke knew that his wife, Faith, was in the country by now, but had not received any recent letter to confirm her actual location. The last letter he had received was over a week ago and she had been commissioned a First Lieutenant on a Direct Commission in San Antonio,

Texas, and had official orders for the Army Hospital in Phu Bai, Vietnam.

Duke hoped that he might get to see Faith should the Battalion be brought back to Camp Eagle for Christmas. He doubted that they would get enough privacy to actually make love, but he longed to see his wife and any time they got to be together would be gratefully accepted and appreciated.

Corporal Turner handed Duke two letters from the mailbag and Duke looked at the return addresses immediately to see who had just written. One letter was from his parents and one letter was from Faith. The return address on Faith's letter indicated the 85th Evacuation Hospital, Phu Bai, Vietnam. Duke immediately opened the letter and began to read:

My Dearest Adam;

Well, I made it to Phu Bai, and I am now a lead shift nurse here at the 85th Evacuation hospital. I was not prepared for the daily onslaught we see here every day. You must be careful my darling as this war has escalated way beyond anything I had expected.

The wounded soldiers we get here every day arrive almost endlessly and most have dreadful wounds and many require amputations. The modern weapons of war are so hideous and the wounds they produce are dreadful. You must be careful darling!

Christmas is just a few days away and I keep hoping that the 1/327th might come back to Camp Eagle to see one of the Christmas shows that have been scheduled here. Our hospital is just around the corner from First Brigade Headquarters, 101st Division on Camp Eagle, as we are co-located with the First Brigade on Camp Eagle.

You will have no trouble finding me, as our operations here are rather large and well marked with signs and a huge Helipad with a red cross to bring in the wounded by helicopter. We listen for the birds all the time as you can hear them approaching the helipad well before they actually arrive.

I hope I get to see you over Christmas. I miss you so much, my darling. Stay safe and come to see me soon.

All my love, Faith

Duke then opened and read the second letter that was from his mother.

Dear Adam,

Faith left for San Antonio in late September according to her parents. They are sick with worry since you are both probably in Vietnam now. Alice Anderson told me that they tried to convince Faith to remain at Fort Benning, but they were unsuccessful in changing her mind. You are both such strong-willed people!

God keep you both safe over there. We want you both back home. This war has become so deadly. The news every night is awful. Your father refuses to watch the evening news on TV, as it is so full of bad news about the war.

The ranch is operating very well this year. We have had a very good calving year on the ranch and most of the newborns are already sold to various huge operations that want the longhorn steers. Your father is ecstatic with the results of his work. The cowboys ask about you often and we have posted a couple of your letters in the main dining room so they can read them for themselves.

Your father is looking forward to the time when you return to the ranch for good. He will never admit it, but ranching is a young man's game and your father, while still strong, cannot work the long days he once loved. We hope that you and Faith will want to take over the ranch once your service obligations are complete. The Double Star Ranch needs both you and Faith here.

The ranch staff continues to grow in size as our operation has expanded beyond any ideas your father and I had ever planned. The town has asked us to sponsor tours to help with the tourism business that brings much-needed income to the town for schools and services. While we want to help in such efforts, it's something entirely foreign to your father's idea of a working ranch so we could use your ideas and recommendations for such a project?

We can hardly wait for this next year to be over and for you to be back in the states. We know you still have another two years of army obligation but we hope that the remainder of your obligation can be spent at a fort in the states, perhaps Fort Hood in Killeen. The ranch needs your help and I know you also want to return to your western roots.

I have sent you a 'goodie box' for Christmas. You can, of course, share it with your platoon. I hope you receive it in time. I really did not know how far ahead to send it and I imagine that the mail will slow down with all the packages being sent for the holidays.

Keep safe son, and come back to us. Love, Mom, and Dad.

Duke laid both letters on top of his rucksack. He would put them both in his ammo can in a few minutes. Each soldier carried their own empty '5.56 caliber M-16 rifle ammunition can' secured by straps under their rucksack. The ammo cans were the perfect size to hold personal items and letters that you did not want to get wet in the jungle. The watertight cans measured about 3 inches by 12 inches by 10 inches and fit well tied with straps under their rucksacks.

Corporal Turner handed the radio to the LT saying, "It's the CO (Company Commander) LT and he wants to talk to you." Duke took the handset and began talking with the CO. They were going to be moved again. Unfortunately, it was not back to Camp Eagle, they were going to relocate to a new Firebase called Firebase Veghel further west toward the Ashau Valley, Vietnam. This was not good news as that area was probably more remote than where they were currently operating.

It was just his luck that his wife was now located at Camp Eagle and the battalion was being shipped further away from Camp Eagle. He just could not get a break! In Duke's mind, this meant that the 1/327th Infantry was not going to any USO show for Christmas. If they were shipping the unit further west it could only mean one thing, the "Above The Rest" 1/327th Infantry was replacing another unit on the absolute front lines allowing that unit to go back to Camp Eagle on stand-down and to see the USO shows. He quietly said as much to his company commander on the radio and CPT Barclay had agreed.

Duke decided not to say anything to his platoon just yet. They were going to be very disappointed and he wanted to think about how he would eventually break the bad news. His RTO, Tim, had heard his side of the conversation with CPT Barclay and he could see the realization in Tim's eyes, but he could trust Tim to say absolutely nothing to anyone. That's preciously one of the reasons he had chosen Tim to be his RTO, Tim understood that all conversations he heard were considered confidential.

Tim had already proved his worth several times in the last two months. He was a quiet and very professional soldier who could be absolutely trusted to keep whatever secrets Duke entrusted to the young man. Tim idolized his young lieutenant almost as if Duke was some kind of rock star instead of a simple Infantry First Lieutenant. Tim took his mission of being the LT's RTO to new levels of professionalism. He saw it as his personal mission in life to make things easier for the LT. They had managed to build a mutual bond that would eventually lead them to an entire lifetime of knowing, working and respecting each other.

Chapter Fifteen: Day Seven Alone
6 April 1970

Duke looked at the handmade calendar and realized that they had been alone in the jungle for a week. It had seemed much longer than that? He was beginning to lose all hope, but he had to keep a good attitude as their very survival might depend on it. Why had the battalion not come to look for them? Obviously, they must think that they were dead and gone. Why else would they abandon two of their own? He was so very dejected.

He also knew that had he not found the extra C-rations in rucksacks left on the LZ, they would probably be dead or in a coma by now. Seven days was a long time to go without good substantial food. The C-rations had literally kept them both alive for the past week but they were running out fast and both men were clearly losing weight. He estimated that if they only ate one C-ration each a day, they might last another two weeks, but then what?

Bananas helped too, but could they stay alive on only bananas? If he decided to go for help and started walking south toward Firebase Veghel, would the banana trees continue? He had no idea how plentiful they were in this area of Vietnam. He had some here in this area, but would they continue as he traveled south? Tim was in no shape to travel and could Duke leave Tim safely behind? He knew the answer to that question was an emphatic 'no'.

The terrible burns on Tim's back were quite evident when Duke had helped to bathe the young man. Both of them had more burns on their backs than anywhere else on their bodies. The explosions and flames had obviously been behind them both and had thrown them both up and forward for over 100 meters.

Duke wondered if he would have permanent scars on the left side of his face from the burns. He could feel the scabs that covered his left cheek and while not a vain man, he did not want to look hideous when he returned to Faith. Then he wondered if he would ever return to Faith. He had to stop such self-depressing thoughts and maintain a bright and cheery attitude, especially for Tim, who appeared to be even more badly wounded than Duke.

Tim was still hanging on, but Duke was beginning to notice changes in Tim that were very disconcerting. The young man withdrew into himself more each day. Duke worried that he was beginning to give up on their situation. Duke could not allow that or he might lose his RTO to death. Duke decided that he had to give a new mission to his sidekick. Tim needed to know that he was valued and that the LT was depending on him. Duke knew that if Tim felt he was doing something to save them both, that Tim would respond well. Duke knew that the young man almost idolized his LT and Duke would need to use that motivation to help keep Tim alive.

He decided to turn over the handmade calendar to his RTO. He turned to Tim and said, "Tim, I need you to take over the keeping of our calendar of days out here in the jungle. It's very important that we know what day it is and how long we have been out here. My headaches are sometimes debilitating and I don't want to make a mistake on the calendar. I need you to keep a clear head and mark down each day."

Tim immediately responded to Duke's request and eagerly took the calendar box from Duke's hands. He then started peppering Duke with questions about Duke's headaches and whether he needed to do anything that might help the LT. The change in Tim's attitude was almost immediate with the simple change in his mission as part of the duo. Duke knew that the young man would respond in kind if he thought his actions were important to the LT.

Duke sat back and took out his map and began looking at possible escape routes out of the jungle. He studied his map carefully. He had to start planning for them both to walk out of here. They could not stay here indefinitely. It was just a matter of time before an enemy patrol or unit would pass by and possibly discover their presence. Then what would happen? They might be killed outright or they might be captured and sent to some God-awful prison in North Vietnam.

Tim would probably not survive such an ordeal. They had to stay hidden until Tim was strong enough to walk. It was probably their best chance for survival and ultimate rescue. Had he been here alone, Duke might have tried walking out of the jungle, but he could not, and would not, leave Tim behind. They would have to survive here until Tim's leg healed enough for him to walk with a crutch.

With that in mind, Duke started looking at his map trying to determine the best routes south that might give them the best chance of success. They could not walk in the lowland areas. They would be too visible to the enemy and even a friendly village could not be assured. The villagers were generally friendly toward the US Army, but some of that was because the units were so strong in numbers.

No village dared to attack a military unit, but two individuals might not be guaranteed support from any local peasants, especially if the Viet Cong (VC) operated anywhere close to the village. The VC soldiers were like the local militia of the communist NVA forces, and generally lived hidden near or among the villages of South Vietnam, either by intimidation or with the village consent.

Being left alone in the wild jungles of Vietnam was almost an automatic death sentence to the average American who had not been raised locally and did not know what was safe to eat and what was not. Americans were so very dependent on their support from their firebases and their rear logistical units.

Food, clothing, ammunition, and fire support all came from the rear support elements. No American unit lived off the land, as in some previous wars. The American Civil War soldier was almost entirely supplied while living off the land, and farms through which the units traveled. But the Civil war was fought inside America and the food available to soldiers was basically the same food they had been raised on. Foreign wars were much different, especially in the Far East where the food was so very different and strange to the average American soldier.

The Asian culture subsisted on rice, fish, and many strange and unknown meat sources and even included dog meat, which was totally repulsive to most Americans. The Vietnam jungle was a totally hostile environment to the average American. What's more, its insects, snakes, monkeys, and food sources were very strange to the average soldier.

That had not always been the case in earlier foreign wars fought by American soldiers in the past, such as Europe, where the US soldier more easily accepted and adapted to the food.

Even the Vietnamese soldiers and people outwardly smelled strongly of garlic, fish, and an especially pungent fish sauce, used on almost all meals. The smells were so very foreign and strong to the average American nose that you could literally smell the NVA soldiers many times before you actually saw the soldiers in the jungle.

Duke already knew that he was losing weight and muscle tone. His fatigues were getting loose and baggy on his body and he knew his strength was waning. But his options were few at this point. Just moving around to get water or the occasional banana took all of his energy. The idea of trying to walk out of this jungle almost fifteen to twenty-five miles seemed almost impossible. Tim continued to deteriorate and slept many hours each day. It was clear that Tim's body had been given a severe jolt and was trying to inwardly repair itself.

Duke knew that the US Air Force flew aircraft every night over the various mountains of South Vietnam using infrared cameras to look for heat sources that might indicate enemy units or activity. He began to formulate a plan to perhaps light a fire in a pit that could only be seen by aircraft at night. This idea came to him when he was war-gaming his possible escape actions.

If he could build a fire on a hilltop that could not be seen from neighboring hilltops, he might be able to signal the US Air Force that he was here without giving away his location to the enemy. But finding and climbing such a hilltop could be nearly as impossible as walking out of here. Building any kind of fire in their current location was absolutely unthinkable as the smoke would just hang over them in the jungle and eventually lead the enemy to their location.

If they wanted to survive, they had to strongly manage their light and noise discipline and keep their presence hidden from any potential enemy, whether that enemy was an NVA, soldier, Viet Cong guerrilla, or a wild animal.

He began looking at his map again and its elevation contour lines with the idea that he had to find the hilltop in this area that was within possible walking distance and would provide such a spot to build such a rescue fire. But even such a fire could pose a threat to their freedom if the smoke traveled to an area where the enemy was located. Any fire could lead the enemy right to their location. He had no working flashlight, as he had found none when he was scrounging for supplies on the LZ after the attack. He continued to rack his brain for rescue ideas until his head actually began to ache again.

He would have to give these ideas some more thought. He also wondered if his 'Home on The Range' message he had written still existed on the LZ since he had not returned to the LZ since the enemy had been there several days ago. He began to think he needed to return to the LZ and ensure that his clues were still visible to any American unit that might land there.

With that in mind, he got himself up, told Tim to stay put, and began to move back to the LZ. He had to make sure that his clues were still visible. It took him another hour to get back to the LZ, and he soon found that the rains had obliterated his message.

He once again wrote the words, adding a new flare to the message. The words now read: "TEXAS, Home on the Range." He looked around and saw no other ration cans or anything that they could use, so he decided to get off the LZ before the enemy might spot him. He then began the climb back to their hiding spot. As he climbed the next hill, he once again heard voices coming from ahead of him.

He immediately moved to the side of the trail and hid in the thickest underbrush he could find. Whoever was coming toward him had evidently already passed by Tim's hiding spot and he hoped they had not discovered him. Within a few seconds, three young men came by his location talking loudly and seemingly enjoying their trek through the jungle. While he saw no weapons among the three men, it was almost certain they were VC guerrillas who routinely maintained contact with the NVA army. Their very presence told Duke that the enemy NVA units were still operating in this area.

Duke quietly waited for almost another hour before he went back to the trail and resumed his trek back to Tim and their hiding place. When he got back to Tim, Tim was wide-awake and tears were streaming down his face. Tim did not say anything to Duke, but it was obvious that leaving Tim alone had been very traumatic to Tim's well being and his psyche. Tim was very fragile and being left alone played on the young man's very being and it was at that moment that Duke knew just how fragile his young friend had become.

Duke would have to curtail his excursions away from their current hiding place to shorter times and more well-defined and explained missions that would not upset Tim's fragile condition. It was now clear to Duke, that Tim actually believed that he was dying and the fear of dying alone was more than the young man could handle.

At that moment Duke understood the one thing that had eluded him until this very day. One of the main reasons that the Vietnam War was not going well for America was the absolute fear among the young soldiers that they were fighting a hopeless cause in a terribly foreign environment to which most of them could not and would not easily assimilate.

Duke took extreme care the rest of the day to reassure Tim that they were going to be rescued and that they would get back home eventually. Tim smiled slightly and showed obvious joy in Duke's reassurance. After all, if the LT said so, then it must be true. Such was the absolute confidence and trust with which Tim held his young lieutenant in his thoughts.

Chapter Sixteen: NVA Attack

Four months earlier

Christmas 1969

Lieutenant Duke Gabriel never did get to see his wife, Faith, over Christmas 1969. His platoon was committed against an NVA suspected Battalion sized force that was trying to attack Firebase Veghel that month. In fact, Duke's platoon had more enemy contact in the month of December than any other month since Duke had arrived in Vietnam.

Several 101st Firebases had come under fire from enemy forces and the First Brigade finally decided to send only token forces to the Christmas celebration shows that were held on Camp Eagle in December 1969. Faith did get to see Bob Hope and his entourage at one of the shows, but she really wanted to see Adam and he never made it to any show.

The NVA attacked four firebases over the Christmas Holiday, including Firebases Nuts, Kathryn, Bastogne, and Veghel. Over 40 soldiers of the 1/327th Battalion were wounded or killed in those attacks. Duke's Platoon had also been ambushed on a trail leading out of the mountains. Fortunately, his point team had been alert and saw the ambush position before the platoon actually entered the 'kill zone'. Duke was able to deploy his platoon in such a manner as to thwart the attack and had actually killed seven NVA soldiers before the NVA unit withdrew and broke all contact, escaping into the jungle.

Duke had learned much in the month of December about survival in the jungle. The rains had come and gone and the jungle just seemed to be more dangerous than usual with enemy forces testing American units at every opportunity. The enemy seemed to be playing with the American units, hitting them with booby traps, mortar attacks from afar, and quick hit and run operations.

Duke had two other firefights with NVA forces in the month of January while patrolling various trails that led out of the mountains and towards the Firebase. In one such contact, Duke's platoon had three men wounded and had to medevac two of them because of serious wounds. His platoon had killed over ten enemy soldiers during those same contacts, but Duke took little pleasure out of the kills when his own soldiers had taken casualties.

The war seemed to be getting even more dangerous since the news from the home front in the states had announced that the American public wanted out of Vietnam. The Stars and Stripes Newspapers carried pictures of demonstrators in almost all editions showing the streets of America full of young people against the war, and the result was demoralizing on his platoon.

By early February, Duke had to work hard to keep his soldiers in line and kept reminding them that they had a war to fight and that their very lives depended upon how well they stayed together and followed their combat discipline. Duke's R&R (Rest and Relaxation) leave was due to come up the next month and he began to wonder if he could just take some in-country leave to be with his wife, Faith, at Camp Eagle instead of leaving Vietnam for Hawaii as most officers did to meet loved ones.

Duke asked his company commander about the possibility of just meeting Faith in Phu Bai, and Captain Barclay said he would find out what options might be given to Duke for his R&R. Duke finally got word back from his commander that he could take his R&R in-country but that finding a place to stay might be a problem for the young couple. Duke immediately wrote to Faith and told her of his dilemma and she assured him that she would find a way they could be together at Camp Eagle.

In the meantime, Duke Gabriel had other things to worry about, as it seemed that the entire area around Firebase Veghel was becoming hot as hell with enemy contact. Duke was well respected by his platoon members and by the higher headquarters, as Duke had become an expert at using Artillery Fire Support, always planning fire support all around his locations. He could call for artillery fires in an instant and protect his platoon from attacking enemy soldiers. Duke had perfected his personal system of artillery protection and took time every day to plan for fires on the surrounding hilltops.

He would constantly call for marker rounds on adjacent hilltops as he moved. By doing this, he could code number each hilltop so that he could call for fire should they come under attack by the enemy. That afternoon, the battalion commander asked Duke to take his platoon to a nearby LZ to receive some visitors. Duke had never "received" any visitors, so this must be some congressman or high "Mucky Muck" that wanted first-hand knowledge of the war.

Duke was not wild about the idea of having some kind of political sightseers traveling with his platoon. He had heard rumors of congressmen and TV crews traveling with platoons but such distractions could get men killed and Duke wanted none of it. But, his company commander told him, that it was not an option and that Duke, "would take these visitors and keep them safe while they were in his care."

Duke moved his platoon to the designated LZ and received the two men. They were a team of reporters from the Associated Press (AP) and they were to move with the platoon for the next three days to see actual troops in action. Duke hated this mission because now he had someone else to take care of that provided no additional firepower to his platoon, and only brought more liability to the unit for their protection.

That evening Duke began his normal routine for planning his night defensive perimeter. His nightly routine rarely varied. He would allow the platoon to form a perimeter and eat supper, and then he would quietly move the platoon some 300 meters away from where they had eaten. This was done so as to confuse any enemy scouts that might have been following his platoon.

Enemy scouts were known to follow platoons to reconnoiter their location since supper always caused the platoon to make excessive noise and Duke knew that the enemy soldiers, if in the area, would hear their preparations for their nighttime security perimeter, an assume that the platoon had settled for the night. Duke would then move the platoon after supper so that if the enemy scouts had been following, they would report back to their commanders with incorrect locations of the platoon for that night.

Duke would then have the platoon quietly go to ground in the new location without digging into the ground so that if they had been followed prior to suppertime, the enemy would no longer know where the platoon was currently located. He would quietly use the radio to call in artillery on the nearby hilltops and would walk the artillery rounds in closer and closer toward the platoon until the shells fragments were actually flying through the trees above their heads. This would bring artillery in close enough to be fatal to any enemy that might try to attack them that evening.

This routine was well known by his soldiers and they understood his tactics and intentions. But the new reporters just thought the young lieutenant was out of his mind and was trying to kill them all with artillery rounds. They demanded to talk to Captain Barclay, the B Company Commander on the radio and told him they wanted to be picked up the next morning as this lieutenant was 'Nuts'.

The next morning Duke was called by his commander and told to take the reporters to an LZ nearby. The two men left the platoon on another helicopter that was sent to pick them up. Duke never did see anything written by the two reporters and no one at Company or Battalion level ever mentioned the incident again.

But no more reporters ever came to Duke's platoon again. Duke's Platoon sergeant slapped Duke on the shoulder as the two reporters got on the helicopter. He said quietly just for Duke to hear, "Good work LT in getting rid of those bastards."

Corporal Turner and the squad leaders thought that the entire incident was terribly funny, and tales would soon be told about the two reporters quick exit for the next six months throughout the entire company. Another Army legend had been started.

Mail call came the next day when they were resupplied by helicopter and a new mailbag arrived. Tim Turner started sorting the mail into stacks for each squad and then turned to Duke, and said, "Hey LT, you got two letters from your wife today! You really hit the jackpot!"

Sure enough, there were two letters from Faith in his hand. He looked at the envelopes wondering which he should open first. He opened the first one and began reading:

Dear Adam: I have secured a guest room here at Camp Eagle for our R&R together this next month. It's actually a set of guest quarters used by the various Generals when they come to visit, but the Hospital Commander has assured me that because March is the month of the quarterly leaders' meetings in Saigon, that it is very unlikely that any General will show up here to bump us out.

I plan to set the room up as a real little love nest and we have been invited to join the Hospital Commander, Colonel Lewis, at his mess table every night if we so desire. It will not be much, darling, but we will be together and that's all that matters to me. I love you darling and want to hold you in my arms again. Please stay safe and come to me, darling.

Your loving wife, Faith.

Duke put down the letter, smiled and opened the second letter:

Dear Adam;

Great news! We can also take a couple of days and go to Eagle beach while you are here. If you can get a jeep from your Battalion we can drive over to Eagle Beach on the coast and have a day there to enjoy the sun and surf which everyone here tells me is just awesome!

Looking forward to your visit, Love Faith.

Duke put down the second note and thought to himself that he just wanted to be with Faith, alone, and naked. He could care less about any beach, but if it made her happy, he would take her to the moon!

Chapter Seventeen: Day Eight Alone
April 1970

Duke awoke to the sound of Tim thrashing about. He immediately tried to calm the young soldier. Duke placed his hand on the forehead of Tim Turner and instantly found that Tim had a fever. What else could possibly go wrong? The next few hours were spent placing wet leaves on Tim's forehead in an attempt to bring his fever down. Duke found some aspirin in one of the first aid kits and fed three to Tim with water.

Duke hoped that the fever was just a mild cold or jungle flu and that it would pass. But he started getting more worried as the day progressed and Tim did not get any better. He managed to get Tim to eat a C-ration meal and Tim seemed to keep the food in his stomach. Duke had fed the meal to Tim spoonful by slow spoonful. Duke was extremely worried. He could lose his sidekick to the flu if he did not improve soon.

Duke wondered if he should try to carry Tim down to the stream to immerse him in the cold water so as to bring his fever down. But then he realized that if he did that, he might not be able to carry him back up the hill. Duke was just not that strong anymore. It was all he could do to get to the stream himself and to get the water they drank every day. If they were stranded by the stream he would be further away from the LZ should any rescue come and they could be much more vulnerable to discovery as the valley below did not have a lot of jungle camouflage. He then poured one of his remaining canteens of water over Tim's body to try and bring down the fever.

If Tim did not improve in the next few hours, he would have to try and get him to the stream the next morning, if Tim lived that long. Duke was very distraught at the thought of losing Tim. He kept searching his thoughts as to what else he might be able to do. He finally started digging a small trench to lay Tim in next to the cool dirt. He finally completed the trench and wet Tim's fatigues and laid the young man in the trench hoping that the cooler earth might bring his fever down. He just had no other ideas of what he might do to save his young RTO.

Meanwhile, back at the Phu Bai 85th Evacuation Hospital, Faith Gabriel tried once again to gain access to the morgue. Yesterday she had come over to the morgue asking questions and had been told that no nurses were allowed into the facility as a safety precaution by the 85th to keep from spreading possible diseases that might be in the morgue.

She had accepted that explanation, but then thought better of it and had sought permission from her commander for her to gain access to the facility to ask some very important questions about her husband. Her immediate commander, Lieutenant Colonel Robert Collins, was an older Medical Service Branch Officer quite out of his element here in Vietnam. Colonel Lewis was the overall commander of the Hospital, but he was away today at a leader's meeting and was not available to talk to about the situation.

LTC Collins, the commander of all of the nurses, was a US Army Reservist thrown into active duty and could not refuse duty in Vietnam if he wanted to salvage his retirement pay when he turned sixty-five years of age. There were many such reservists and doctors serving in Vietnam against their own better judgment and family wishes.

But LTC Collins was a pleasant family man and immediately took sympathy on the young widow standing in front of him today. After talking with Faith for over thirty minutes, he acquiesced, and gave Faith permission to enter the morgue to ask some questions. He then accompanied Faith over to the morgue to help her gain entrance to the facility.

They entered the morgue, which smelled strongly of ammonia and formaldehyde. It was almost too overwhelming. Faith asked the young lieutenant at the front of the morgue where she could see the report of the 1/327th LZ attack last week? The lieutenant took note of the Lieutenant Colonel accompanying the young female officer, and immediately got up and escorted them to the rear of the facility.

Once further back into the morgue area, the lieutenant introduced the pair to the Morgue Watch Officer, a Captain Hardy, and the young lieutenant then returned to his post at the front of the morgue. Captain Hardy listened to Faith's request and sent his First Sergeant in search of the records involving the 1/327th Infantry. The three officers then sat and talked while the First Sergeant was gone. Faith informed the young Captain that she was married to Lieutenant Adam Gabriel and just happened to be serving at the 85th Hospital.

Captain Hardy said he had never before met the spouse of a deceased military member in Vietnam, and said that he was very sorry for her loss. They talked a few moments about the current state of the war before the First Sergeant returned with the file. He handed the file to Captain Hardy, who in turn then handed the file to LTC Collins.

LTC Collins opened the file and began reading. He wanted to spare Faith if the file contained any gruesome details about her husband's wounds or death. After looking at the file for a couple of minutes, he then handed the file to Faith. LTC Collins then looked at

Captain Hardy and asked why the file did not contain any results of the autopsy of Lieutenant Gabriel?

Captain Hardy was surprised and asked what the Colonel meant? Lieutenant Colonel Collins said that page two of the report listed Lieutenant Gabriel and Corporal Turner, but no autopsy results were listed for either man. Captain Hardy then took the file from Faith and looked at the file himself. Captain Hardy, who was not a physician, did not review every file of every death, as there were just too many such deaths for him to review them all.

He studied all of the papers in the file for a few more minutes and then sent his First Sergeant to get the sergeant who had filed the papers. The next thirty minutes were spent with several people who had helped in the autopsies of the men from the 1/327th LZ explosions. It became obvious very quickly that none of the doctors had known that there were supposed to be twelve men from the horrific scene as the file contained results on only ten autopsies, six enlisted men of D Company, 1/327th Infantry, and four Warrant Officer pilots.

Faith asked her commander for permission to go to the 1/327th and brief the Battalion Commander about the findings. LTC Collins said that he would gladly accompany her to the infantry headquarters just down the road, as he felt this was a mistake of grave proportions and he should be there too. Obviously, there were two men missing in action whose bodies were never retrieved. LTC Collins felt it was almost impossible for there not to be some kind of body evidence retrieved from the explosion site.

If true, then two men were unaccounted for and their bodies were possibly still out in the jungle somewhere, either dead or waiting for rescue. No one at the morgue could ever remember such a thing as happening before. It was clearly an administrative oversight of grave possible consequence.

LTC Collins called for his driver and vehicle to be brought around the front of the hospital and Faith and LTC Collins headed for the 1/327th Infantry Rear Area Headquarters just up the road from the hospital. They arrived at about 1600 hours (4 PM) and immediately asked to speak to the commander.

Major Garvey, the Battalion Executive Officer and the Rear Detachment Commander saw them and asked if they would like some coffee? The three of them sat in Major Garvey's office and LTC Collins began by saying, "Major Garvey, we have just today learned that the number of identified bodies from the LZ explosion of last week does not match with all of the names provided to the morgue.

Major Garvey leaned forward and said, "I'm sorry, what do you mean that the autopsies do not match the soldiers?" LTC Collins once again said, "Well, you had provided us with a casualty report containing twelve men's names, but our autopsies can only identify and account for ten bodies." Major Garvey then said, "Could the remaining two have been completely destroyed or vaporized?"

LTC Collins said, "Possibly, but it has never happened before, as there is usually some body parts submitted to the morgue. What I am telling you is that no body part was evidently matched to two of the men on the casualty report."

Major Garvey said, "Who are the soldiers which are missing?" LTC Collins said quietly, "Lieutenant Adam Duke Gabriel and Corporal Timothy Turner are missing. Lieutenant Gabriel's wife, Faith, who is with me today, is assigned to the 85th Evacuation Hospital and so, of course, she was curious and she actually discovered the mistake."

Major Garvey stood and said, "My God, I am so sorry LT, this must be absolutely terrible for you?" Faith spoke for the first time, and said, "Actually, Major Garvey, I am thrilled at this news because perhaps my husband is still alive somewhere out near that LZ. Wouldn't that be just great?"

LTC Collins and Faith then returned to the hospital as Major Garvey went to the Rear Detachment Operations center to call his boss, LTC Brody, out on Firebase Veghel. Major Garvey told the battalion commander about his visitors and LTC Brody said, "My God, you mean that two of our soldiers could still be out there?" Major Garvey said, "Yes sir, they could be still out there somewhere near the LZ or perhaps they were killed and blown off the LZ into the jungle somewhere. At any rate, we absolutely know that none of the recovered body remains matched the LT nor his RTO".

LTC Brody looked at his watch and then said, "Well, it will be dark in just a couple of hours, so we won't be able to get back out there tonight before dark, but I will alert the Air Force to fly a SLAR (Side Looking Airborne Radar) Mission over that LZ tonight." If they are alive, perhaps the SLAR will pick up their body heat with their infrared cameras? We can mount a rescue mission first thing in the morning using the Tiger Force".

The Tiger Force was an elite platoon of well-experienced men led by a handpicked Lieutenant that was used by the battalion as its eyes and ears when needed. It was a stand-alone unit that reported directly to the Battalion Operations Officer (S-3) and the Battalion Commander. They wore a special uniform that had 'tiger stripes' set on top of black camouflage uniforms and they were used as a rescue force or as a reconnaissance force as may be needed by the battalion. They were all extremely experienced soldiers on their second or third tour of duty in Vietnam and led by a hand picked officer.

The Battalion Commander immediately alerted his Operations Officer to begin planning to insert the Tiger Force onto LZ 786 first thing in the morning to look for Lieutenant Gabriel and his RTO who might still be alive or dead in the area. This set into motion quite a few actions that would take most of the night to get accomplished. The Tiger Force would first have to be extracted from wherever they were currently operating and then resupplied. They would then have to be briefed for this new mission and helicopters would have to be ordered for tomorrow to insert the resupplied Tiger Force into the new area.

Such an operation would require many people working all night long to get everything working and set into motion. Everyone in the operations center was on high alert. The idea that two American soldiers could have been left alive on LZ 786 motivated everyone to get this operation back out to LZ 786.

Chapter Eighteen: Vietnam – R&R

One Month Earlier

March 1970

Duke took his R&R in March 1970 at Camp Eagle Vietnam for six days at the Phu Bai Hospital. No one could ever remember anyone taking an in-country R&R at the First Brigade Headquarters at Camp Eagle. Faith had been true to her word and had secured a private guest suite at the Hospital where the lovebirds could reside for the week. She also managed to work a lot of time off by trading future nursing shifts with other nurses at the hospital.

As it finally turned out, the couple had a second honeymoon hidden away at Camp Eagle. It was the perfect compliment to the one they had spent in the guest cabin at the ranch the year before. They were both temporarily out of their jobs and in a place they had never been before. They spent their entire time exploring each other's bodies and making love as many times as physically possible in any twenty-four hour period.

Duke and Faith would pledge their entire lives and bodies to each other for as long as they both would live. There was something about making love and being so intimate together in a live and active combat zone with the sounds of artillery shells firing in the background to raise the stakes of their very existence. They knew that they had been given a special gift to be together here in Vietnam. They also knew that the war could take it all away in the next month or any month thereafter until they returned to the states. It made their time together mean so much more than any regular vacation together.

The Hospital Commander, Col Lewis had been good to his word and had arranged the Military Guest Suite for the honeymooners and they were his personal guests at his mess table every night for the week that Duke spent at Camp Eagle. It was a wonderful experience for them both and Duke was so glad that things had finally worked out for them to be together for such a wonderful experience.

Duke had managed to secure a jeep from the company supply officer, Captain Ted Severn, at the rear detachment of Company D who fancied himself the best scrounger in all of Vietnam. The couple then used the jeep to ride out to Eagle Beach near Da Nang for two of their afternoons where they could sun themselves and enjoy the surf at the in-country R&R facility used by various units. For Adam, it was sheer heaven to be once again in Faith's arms and both enjoyed each other's company for the week.

While they were at Eagle Beach the wildest thing had happened. Unbeknownst to Lt Gabriel, the 1/327th Battalion had decided to send his First Platoon to Eagle Beach for a two day pass since their Lieutenant was away on R&R and the Battalion Commander did not like leaving platoons in the jungle where they might get into action without their normal leadership team being complete.

An Eagle Beach slot had come open for a platoon and LTC Brody saw it as a perfect opportunity to give the platoon a good time while their lieutenant was away on R&R. He had not counted on Lieutenant Gabriel being at the beach at the same time, as he thought Duke and Faith were back at Camp Eagle.

So, Lieutenant Colonel Brody had sent Duke's First Platoon to Eagle beach for two days with SFC Bell. Faith and Duke were sunning themselves on the beach when a platoon of soldiers came running onto the beach screaming and hollering. As the platoon got closer, Duke Gabriel just about lost his cool, as the young men clustered around the young lieutenant and his wife yelling and screaming about finding their LT on the beach with his absolutely beautiful blond wife!

Duke introduced his beautiful bride to the platoon and the next several hours were spent with the men congratulating the LT on his beautiful bride and with telling him how lucky he was. Tim, his RTO, took particular interest in his bride, Faith, and sat right next to her on the beach to tell her all about how impressed he was with Lieutenant Gabriel and how lucky she was to have such a fantastic man. It was all a little embarrassing to Duke.

SFC Bell finally intervened and told all the soldiers to leave the LT to enjoy his R&R and took the men to the other side of the beach to set up a volleyball game. Duke turned to Faith, and sheepishly said, “I swear I had no idea that they would be here today.” Faith just laughed and said, “Well, I guess I just have to learn to be able to share you with the entire world,” as she pulled his mouth towards hers and kissed him on the lips.

The rest of the day was absolute bliss as they enjoyed the sun and the surf. The day was made that much better for Duke, as knowing that his platoon was here on the beach and not back in the jungle took his mind off having to worry about his platoon being without his leadership. It was a win-win situation.

They thoroughly enjoyed their time together and it seemed that the R&R came to an end much too soon for them both. But they had managed to discuss their future and both agreed that once they returned to the states, they wanted to try and finish any remaining obligations to the army through a local reserve unit near Odessa as they really wanted to live at the Double Star ranch and start their lives together as ranchers as soon as possible.

They both missed their horses, and the western lifestyle they had grown up with and wanted to reconnect with family and the land. On their final night together at the Hospital, Duke managed to get a great table at the very small but comfortable Camp Eagle Officers Club and they had a wonderful steak dinner together alone. It was hard to believe they were sitting in an Officers Club in a combat zone in the middle of Vietnam.

Duke left the next morning in the jeep he had brought to the hospital and drove it back to the D Company Rear Area and was back in his platoon the next afternoon. His platoon had been placed on Firebase security after they had returned from Eagle Beach and the soldiers were rather glad that they could get hot showers and hot meals for the days that their LT was gone on his R&R.

SFC Bell was glad to see the young Lieutenant again as he liked his normal duties of Platoon Sergeant and he was not fond of dealing with everything that the LT did daily. He was smiling broadly as the LT took back the reins of the platoon and they then prepared to leave the firebase for their next mission location.

The platoon members had gained a new respect for their young officer when they saw his wife at Eagle Beach. The rumors now ran rampant throughout the platoon about how lucky he was to have such a beautiful woman on his arm and they had all decided that he was really such a stud! His RTO Tim now held him to almost God-like proportions. They all felt so fortunate to have such a man's man be their platoon leader in Vietnam.

The next morning the platoon was inserted back into the jungle west of Firebase Veghel. Everything reverted back to normal operations and Duke was back into his combat role of combat commander. He spent the next several days ensuring that the platoon was back up to the standards he expected and the unit went back to operating efficiently and professionally.

Just as before he had left on R&R, he soon discovered that Vietnam was becoming hotter every day as the enemy began in earnest to harass them at every turn available. Two nights after returning to the jungle, the platoon was involved in a firefight with an unknown size force and his RTO, Corporal Turner actually saved Duke's life when an enemy soldier broke through their perimeter defenses and rushed the command post.

As the enemy soldier rushed toward the lieutenant and lifted his AK 47 rifle towards Lieutenant Gabriel, Tim Turner pushed his lieutenant over and then opened fire with his M-16 set on automatic mode and put some twenty M-16 rounds through the chest of the attacking enemy soldier.

The enemy soldier fell onto the ground right in front of them both. Had Corporal Turner not noticed the enemy soldier breaking through their security perimeter when he did, they would both probably be dead right now. Lieutenant Gabriel looked over at the young Corporal and stammered to say, “Thank you”. Tim just smiled and said, “No sweat LT, it's just another day in the Nam!”

Such was the bond of brotherhood that had grown between Corporal Tim Turner and his young lieutenant. Tim had taken on the personal responsibility to be a bodyguard against any enemy attempt to kill his LT. Tim was now a hero in the platoon and was recommended and awarded the Bronze Star for valor for that action.

Chapter Nineteen: Day Nine Alone
April 1970

The day started out rather badly. Tim's fever was getting worse, and Duke was at his wit's end as to what to try to make the young soldier any more comfortable. Duke felt that the Corporal was dying. He kept giving water in small sips to the young man who was clearly in trouble and no longer recognized or acknowledged Duke's presence.

Meanwhile, back at Firebase Veghel, the Tiger Force was preparing for insertion back onto LZ 786. LTC Brody had gotten a report from the US Air Force from last night's flyover missions and it said that they had detected two 'Hot Spots" on the hilltop slightly south and next to the LZ. This usually meant that two men or possibly two animals were on that hilltop. LTC Brody personally briefed Lieutenant 'Buck' Cannon, the platoon leader of the Tiger Force, about the Air Force 'Side Looking Radar Report.'

Buck had been on LZ 786 just the week before when they first recovered the bodies. He had felt that they had retrieved all of the bodies and was very distressed that they might have missed anyone. He vowed to find the two men and to rescue them. The

Tiger Force loaded out their helicopters and lifted off Firebase Veghel headed for Hill 786.

Duke had just about decided that he would have to try and get Tim to the stream. His fever had not abated and Duke was afraid that if it continued at this rate, the young man would be dead by suppertime tonight. How could things get any worse? He got the answer to that question in the next fifteen minutes. As he sat next to Tim putting wet leaves on Tim's head, he heard noises coming from the trail to their east. Something or someone was coming up the trail.

Duke whispered to Tim to try and stay silent but he did not know if Tim could even hear him. He then gathered their available grenades and his pistol and laid out the extra two magazines of ammo for his 45-caliber pistol. The grenades, his pistol, and the two extra magazines were all he had to defend them both against any enemy attack. He wondered how long he could hold out against any real enemy force? He'd be lucky to take a few enemy soldiers with him, but he and Tim would most probably die in any such shootout.

It was all he had, and he would have to make each weapon count if they were discovered. He sat next to the tree and listened to the approaching noise. It was definitely a human being, at least one, maybe more. He then heard their voices and confirmed that they were Vietnamese. The worst was about to happen; as they would soon be discovered as several of the enemy soldiers were walking on the flanks of the enemy column coming directly toward Duke's hiding place.

At the same time that he heard the approaching patrol, he could also hear helicopters approaching from above. The enemy patrol stopped and began talking rapidly together. They had obviously heard the same helicopters approaching and were probably trying to determine what they should do. At that very moment, an enemy soldier came off the trail and walked right up to Duke apparently without even seeing him sitting next to the tree.

Duke took aim and fired one shot from his pistol and hit the young soldier dead center chest. He then immediately threw a grenade behind the soldier and toward the trail where Duke estimated the rest of the enemy column was located. The grenade exploded into the loudest and biggest explosions that Duke had ever seen or heard from any one grenade.

Unbeknownst to Lieutenant Gabriel, the grenade had exploded next to a stretcher that was being carried by two enemy soldiers. The stretcher was filled with explosive satchel charges, which then exploded when the grenade went off almost immediately underneath the stretcher. The entire jungle went up in flames and the blast was enormous.

Duke then threw two more grenades and fired the rest of his 45caliber pistol magazine in the direction of the enemy hoping the enemy soldiers would think there were more US soldiers with Duke.

Duke thought that the first grenade he had thrown had to be the strongest grenade he had ever seen in his life. He sat there dumbfounded beyond belief. At the same moment, American helicopters started landing on LZ 786 and unloading the fierce Tiger Force, which had just seen the explosions on the next hilltop. Lieutenant Cannon had already called for gunship support and was directing the gunships towards the next hilltop.

Duke could hear the very distinct whop-whop-whop of the two bladed Cobra gunships above and knew they were about to commence firing on the hilltop where he currently sat with Tim. Duke had to let the pilots know that there were friendlies on the hilltop. He crawled over to the rucksack and pulled out the one green smoke grenade that he had brought with him from the LZ, pulled the pin, and threw it into the brush just a few meters from where he sat. The green smoke started to climb up through the brush and trees on the wind.

He then slammed another magazine into his pistol, and began firing again and threw another explosive grenade that he had been saving for any possible combat action they might encounter. Within minutes he had exhausted all of his available ammunition with the exception of one grenade that he could use if the enemy converged on top of he and Tim. He did not intend for them to be taken alive and be tortured. He would rather end it all and take the enemy with him than to die in some rat hole of a North Vietnam prison.

The Cobra gunship commander immediately saw the green smoke billowing up from the jungle and told his gunships to evade firing anywhere too close to the green smoke, a well-known signal of friendly forces. The Cobras were on the same radio frequency as Lieutenant Cannon and the cobra commander started asking the Tiger Force who was on the adjacent hilltop. Lieutenant Cannon told the cobra commander that he could only assume it was Lieutenant Duke Gabriel.

The next hour was sheer pandemonium as Duke held tight to his one last grenade hoping that he would not have to use it. The Cobra gunships circled the green smoke and began firing outside of what they considered the friendly force on top of the hill. Duke was mesmerized. The Cobras were protecting he and Tim without any radio contact from Duke. It was truly a miracle. The enemy force had obviously been badly wounded by the huge explosions and whoever remained alive must have 'beat feet' in the other direction as the Cobras arrived on the scene.

Within the hour, the Tiger Force managed to make its way to Duke Gabriel and Tim's hiding position. Duke knew Lieutenant Cannon personally and was so very glad to see him approach their little hideaway. The young lieutenant then pulled back a bit as he said, "My God Man, you guys need a bath!" They both laughed and Duke said, "You would not smell so good either if you had been through what we have in the past week. Duke then told Buck that he had to call a medevac immediately, as he thought that Tim was dying.

The Tiger force had brought two stretchers and they set about lifting Tim on one and began moving him back to the LZ quickly for medevac. Buck then moved forward and helped Duke stand up and asked him if he wanted a stretcher? Duke said that he probably should, as he was not very strong anymore. Buck got Duke on the stretcher and actually helped to carry him back to the LZ as the Tiger Force, under the direction of their Platoon Sergeant, began scouring the jungle for any leftover enemy soldiers. There were enemy bodies everywhere.

By the time Duke and Buck got back to the LZ, the medevac bird had already taken Tim from the LZ and everyone was coming back to the LZ for extraction. The Tiger Force Platoon Sergeant reported back that the explosion caused by Duke's grenades and the accompanying explosions from the enemy satchel charges had killed some ten enemy soldiers and one soldier had been shot dead through the chest.

The Tiger platoon sergeant turned to LT Duke Gabriel and said, "My God LT, you must be a relative of Sergeant Alvin York, from Tennessee, as you took on over a dozen enemy soldiers all by yourself and killed them all! Duke looked up at the young sergeant and said, "Well, I always have been able to hit at whatever I aimed at!" They all laughed as the birds began coming to the LZ for the extraction. Duke looked up at Lieutenant Buck Cannon and said, "Damn Buck, you sure took long enough to come and get me?" Buck looked back at the skinny lieutenant on the stretcher and said, "Sorry man, we had no idea you were left here in the first place." Duke was sent out on the next bird with four soldiers from the Tiger Force.

It was the best helicopter ride Duke Gabriel had ever experienced. Lying on the stretcher and being among the elite soldiers of the Tiger Force warmed his heart. They had not forgotten about him and they did come back for him. He was very thankful and sent up a small prayer to God for sending the Tiger Force to get he and Tim. He hoped Tim would make it.

Duke and Tim were both taken to the 85th Evacuation Hospital, where they were immediately put on intravenous transfusions of liquids and nutrients. LTC Brody visited Duke that very evening at the hospital and personally apologized for leaving he and Tim in the jungle. Duke thought it was a very nice gesture but informed the Colonel that there was no way that he could have known just what happened that day on the extraction of Duke's platoon. The Colonel finally acknowledged Duke's words but said that he felt bad just the same.

LTC Brody recommended Duke for the Silver Star for his actions against the enemy near LZ 786 and recommended Tim for the Bronze Star for the same action and both men were recommended for the Army Soldier's Medal for saving each other's lives. Duke and Tim would be awarded several awards while recuperating in the hospital for the next month.

Faith and Duke were reunited at the 85th and Duke hugged her so tight that Faith finally had to say, "You're crushing me darling", to which he said, "I don't ever want to let you go". They spent most of the day together as Duke alternately slept and just enjoyed the clean sheets, bath, pain medicine, and soup he had been given. His face would carry a few permanent scars but Faith assured him that it just made him look more rugged!

He asked several times how Tim was doing and was told each time that the young Corporal was doing OK, but it was good that they got him to the hospital when they did, as his pneumonia was serious and he could well have died without treatment with antibiotics.

They told Duke that Tim had contracted pneumonia and not the flu as Duke had thought, and it was just a matter of time before his lungs would have filled with fluid, and he would have suffocated and succumbed to the disease had he stayed in the jungle. Duke was so glad that the Tiger Force had returned for them.

He would later find out that had it not been for his lovely wife, Faith, they might not have been found in time to save Tim from pneumonia. Heaven only knows if Duke would have survived to try to walk some fifteen to twenty-five miles to Firebase Veghel after Tim's death. He certainly would not have attempted it with Tim still alive. Both of their lives had been saved because Faith had the presence of mind to start asking questions.

Duke then thought back to Faith's decision to come to Vietnam as a nurse. Had she not been determined to serve her country like her husband, Duke may have never made it back home. Duke was so emotionally drained that he had a hard time expressing his thoughts to Faith, as she sat there next to him holding his hand. He finally just looked at her as a single tear ran down his face. Faith got up and cradled his battered face in both of her hands and lightly kissed him. Duke Gabriel knew that God had saved he and Tim, using Faith, both the woman, and his faith in God!

Duke and Tim spent the rest of the month at the 85th Evacuation and were then transferred to Madigan Medical Center in Washington State, USA, for several more surgeries and skin grafts each treating their extensive burns on their backs, faces, and arms and their broken leg injuries. Faith stayed in Vietnam until the end of her tour in May, and then returned home to Fort Benning to await the arrival of Duke from Madigan Medical Center in Washington State.

Duke and Tim were roomed together at Madigan Hospital because of their mutual requests, and had become almost inseparable since their ordeal together. Duke learned a lot about Tim while they were recuperating together at Madigan. He learned that Tim had joined the army to get out of an extremely abusive home where his father had beat both he and his mother. That his mother had "fallen down the stairs" and was pronounced dead by the responding medics after Tim had called 911, when he was only 17 years of age.

Tim blamed his father for his mother's death, but there were no eyewitnesses to the accident and when Tim returned home from High School that day, he found his mother lying in blood at the foot of the stairs. Duke was told that Tim's father was not in the home when Tim found his mother. Tim believed that his father had killed her either by pushing her or beating her to the point that she stumbled to the stairs and fell. Of course, Tim could not prove anything and his father had warned him after the “accident” that he had better not say anything, or he too might sustain a fall.

Tim would never return to that house, deciding to immediately join the army instead. Tim never wanted to see his father again. He felt his father had killed his mother and suspected that his father had been in the house when the accident occurred. But his father had been cleared of any wrongdoing by the authorities because his mother had never voiced any complaints to the police while she was still alive. If Tim were to try and lay blame to his father it might not be true and worse yet, it could have delayed Tim from joining the Army.

Tim hated his father and would never forgive him for the continued abuse in their home. He had joined the army and never looked back. He told Duke he had no college education but that he did want to take some courses someday to better himself. He never wanted to end up like his father, uneducated, and bitter about his lot in life. He hoped to use some of his Army GI Bill benefits to enroll in college after his time in the army.

Both men were kept at Madigan Hospital for over two months for several burn surgeries each, and rehabilitation. They were also told that their injuries were considered too severe to continue on active duty in the infantry, as neither one of them would ever probably walk normally again. Both were to be medically discharged sometime in the next month. They would then get more medical assistance as may be needed from their local VA hospitals.

Duke asked Tim if he had ever considered working on a ranch? Tim said that he like horses, but he had never been given an opportunity to work around them as he was growing up. Duke offered Tim a job on the Double Star Ranch in Texas, and Tim said he would love the opportunity, as he had nowhere else to go and no family to return home to. Duke was determined to help the young man get a good start in life. Duke felt so blessed in his home, wife, and family and just could not imagine the home where young Tim Turner had grown up.

Both men were discharged from the hospital on June 10th, 1970 after a joint promotion ceremony in their hospital room. Lieutenant Adam Gabriel was promoted to Captain, and Corporal Tim Turner was promoted to Sergeant E5, (Buck Sergeant) in the US Army. The hospital commander promoted Duke and Duke then promoted Tim. After the promotion ceremony, Duke took Tim aside and gave him a credit card with Duke's name on it.

He told Tim to use the credit card to buy food and transportation to Dallas, Texas, and to then take a bus from Dallas to Odessa, Texas. He gave him the phone number to the Double Star Ranch and told him that Dwayne Hobbs, the Ranch Foreman, had already been told to expect a call from Tim when he got to Odessa.

Hobbs would pick him up at the bus station and get him to the ranch. Once at the ranch, Tim was to turn the credit card over to Hobbs and begin his life as a new Ranch Hand. He told Tim that Hobbs was a very good man and that he should follow his lead. He then told Tim Turner that he would join him at the ranch once he had cleared his quarters at Fort Benning.

Duke had to return to Fort Benning and to his wife, Faith, and their army quarters and would be actually discharged at Fort Benning and not at Madigan Hospital with Tim. Tim could be discharged right from the hospital. He told Tim that they would see him at the ranch after they packed out their household goods and left Fort Benning. Tim was flabbergasted! No one had ever trusted him with such responsibility before and he was so very thankful for Duke's trust in him.

Their fated meeting in Vietnam would lead to a lifelong friendship, as Tim Turner would travel to the Double Star Ranch, become a trusted member of the ranch, and eventually become a part owner in the spread with Duke and his brother Billy some ten years later.

Tim would also attend the local community college using his GI Bill benefits and eventually obtain a BS degree in business.

EPILOGUE: The Ranch

One year later

Duke sat on his horse, Rustler, and looked out over the Double Star Ranch. Tim Turner had made it to the ranch and Hobbs was so impressed with the young man that he had made him a lead wrangler and trail boss for the upcoming roundup of cattle for market.

Duke and Faith had moved into the main house with Duke's little brother Billy and Faith had turned the place into her own home. Billy was to leave for college soon and was debating whether he would join ROTC and follow Duke's lead. Duke's parents had moved into the Guest Cabin and had added an addition to the cabin that included a sunroom, bigger kitchen and many extras to make it the ideal retirement home for them both.

Faith was now almost eight months pregnant and was expecting a healthy boy to be delivered the next month. They were still debating over what to name the new boy and the naming conversations had taken on a rather festive atmosphere all over the ranch as everyone on the ranch had another idea as to just what to name the boy. It was clear that he was going to be loved by all when he finally arrived.

Duke looked up at the sky and saw the same kind of clouds he had seen so many times in Vietnam when he was wondering if he and Tim would live to get back home. He thanked God for his blessings, for Faith, for Tim, and for this wonderful ranch that he now called home.

He then looked at his Rolex watch and decided that he had to head back to the main house. Faith was planning a great dinner tonight for the one-year anniversary of Tim and Duke returning home from Vietnam.

Faith had also invited a young lady friend she had met in town and wanted to introduce her new young friend Elizabeth to Tim Turner at dinner. Ever the matchmaker, Faith was intent to eventually find just the right mate and match for Tim, as he badly needed his own stable family. Tim deserved to have love in his life as she and Duke had together and Faith was bound and determined to find the right gal.

Duke laughed inwardly as he rode back to the main ranch house, as he just knew that Tim was going to be completely tongue-tied tonight at dinner when he saw Elizabeth who was a charming and beautiful young lady.

(This photo was self-taken by Auto-tripod)

Gary L Gresh is a retired U.S. Army Colonel who lives in the village of Flat Rock, North Carolina. This is his eleventh book and he is currently working on two more.

Gary is a historian by heart and education and loves the historical novel format as a means to bring history and romance alive to today's audience. All of his books are available in both Amazon Kindle and Paperback editions, all available on Amazon.com. He strives to get the history correct, while his fictional characters are usually both very real, romantic, and usually based on actual people Gary has met throughout his long life.

He is a graduate of Washington and Jefferson College with a BA in History and has two advanced degrees, including The United States Army War College. His passion for American history and the US Civil War era has also led him to collect civil war memorabilia and to writing about the Post Civil War West.

He and his wife of 51 years, Barbara, moved to Flat Rock after his 30-year career as a Paratrooper in the US Army.

A distinguished Officer, he served in many Army Special Operations Units in two different branches of the Army and was awarded over 24 Army awards during his career.

He commanded an Infantry platoon and Company in Vietnam, a Special Forces A-Team in Germany, a Battalion at Fort Jackson, S.C. and a Brigade sized unit of the 18th Airborne Corps in Operation Desert Storm in 1990-91.

His awards include the Distinguished Flying Cross, Two Bronze Stars, and The United States Army Distinguished Service Medal awarded by the Secretary of The Army upon his retirement as the Nation's 20th Commandant of the Adjutant General Corps in 1998.

Colonel Gresh is also a 2011 inductee in the US Army's AGC Hall of Fame for his distinguished service to the US Army from 1968-1998.

CPSIA information can be obtained
at www.ICGtesting.com
Printed in the USA
LVHW011713020419
612699LV00018B/826